THE GAME MASTER
Mansion Mystery

THE GAME MASTER

MANSION MYSTERY

BY MATT & REBECCA ZAMOLO

ILLUSTRATIONS BY CHRIS DANGER

HARPER

An Imprint of HarperCollinsPublishers

Library of Congress Control Number: 2021949050
ISBN 978-0-06-302513-4

Typography by Chris Kwon
22 23 24 25 26   PC/LSCH   10 9 8 7 6 5 4 3 2 1
❖
First Edition

THE GAME MASTER
Mansion Mystery

CHAPTER 1

Becca

Becca Zamolo stood in the corner of the treehouse with her arms crossed, looking over her group of friends as they passed around a bag of chips. Their meeting was supposed to start five minutes ago, but they were still missing one person—Miguel, who was the least likely of them all to show up late. Something about it made Becca feel weird.

"Where is he?" Becca wondered out loud, biting her lip. "Miguel is always on time, like, to *everything*."

"Chill out, Becks," Matt said through a mouthful, spitting bits of chips over the front of his shirt as he spoke. "He'll be here soon."

"Totally," Kylie agreed. "I talked to him yesterday about

the meeting and he said he'd definitely be here."

But something still didn't sit right in Becca's stomach. Maybe it was because ever since she and her group of friends were summer schooled by the mysterious Game Master two months ago, Becca felt paranoid about everything: windows that she didn't remember opening, unexpected knocks on the front door, even the innocent little notes her mother would leave her in her lunchbox. None of these things ended up actually being caused by the Game Master, but they still always left Becca with a lump in her throat and a racing heart.

"You're right." Becca finally gave in, taking a seat between Kylie and Danny, who was messing around with his camera like always, zooming in on Matt and his sharklike chomping of the chips. "I think I just need to relax."

"You've got that right," Matt answered, winking so Becca would know that he was kidding, as if ninety percent of the things that came out of his mouth weren't a joke. "Make like a cucumber and chill, Becks."

Before the summer school incident, Becca could hardly stand her longtime neighbor Matt, whose mother was best friends with Becca's mother. But something about that wild day where they were locked in their school together with Kylie, Danny, Frankie, and Miguel, all at the mercy of the elusive Game Master, changed how Becca and Matt looked at each other. They were becoming something closer to best friends themselves.

"So, interview time while we wait for Miguel," Danny said, pointing the camera at Frankie this time. "Frankie, how do you feel about the fact that we still haven't been able to find Elephant?"

Elephant belonged to Miguel's little brother, Angel. The day the group beat the Game Master and figured out all the clues necessary to break out of the locked school, they came home to find that the game was far from over. Elephant had been kidnapped, and the Game Master had left a note in his place:

You may have won the first round, my friends. But stay alert. Because the games have just begun.
—GM

Frankie swallowed their chips and looked into the camera with sad eyes. "Terrible," they said after a dramatic pause. "I can only take solace in the fact that whoever this twisted Game Master is, they at least seem to be taking care of Elephant, you know, despite the whole *hamster-napped* thing."

It was true. Even though the group of newly bonded pals hadn't received any other clues that might help them locate the missing hamster, the Game Master had been sending them all photos of Elephant in different outfits, looking fed and well taken care of. Still, knowing that Elephant was okay hadn't made any of this easier for Miguel. He had to stop sharing the photos with Angel after the third or fourth one because it would always make him cry out of worry for his beloved pet.

"Seriously," Kylie piped in, and Danny swooped his camera over to get her in the shot. "Who kidnaps a hamster? For *two months*? If this was intended to be a game, it's gone way too far."

"I think we already passed the 'too far' point when we caught Mr. Verdi at the school last time," Matt added, and Danny expertly moved the camera from Kylie's face to Matt's. "Remember how he started sobbing when we confronted him?"

"But Mr. Verdi wasn't the Game Master," Becca pointed out, raising her chin just the slightest bit. When the camera moved to her face, she straightened her back and cleared her throat. "He was just somebody who got caught in the game. Remember what he told us? The Game Master made him do all that stuff."

"Nobody makes grownups do anything they don't want to do," Frankie scoffed. "I still think Mr. Verdi is suspicious as heck."

Becca couldn't exactly deny it. Ever since the new school year started, Mr. Verdi had been missing from campus, which wasn't exactly innocent behavior. Could it be true that Mr. Verdi had known more than he let on that day?

The entire thing was so confusing. The Game Master was calculating enough to have planned the summer school incident without issue, from clues hidden with glow-in-the-dark stickers to puzzles that honed in on each kid's special interest in one way or another. And a flyer had been left behind describing each one of them to a T. It was almost as if the Game Master had wanted to be their friends, but what kind of friend would put a group of kids through such wild challenges?

"Well, whoever it is, we're going to find out," Becca finally said, breaking the awkward silence that had come over them all at the mention of Mr. Verdi. "Trust me when I say that. We killed it last time around, so whenever the Game Master decides to throw us a bone in helping us find Elephant, we'll be ready."

"Agreed," Kylie and Frankie said simultaneously, which caused them to crack up at each other.

"I think things are getting a little too serious at this particular meeting," Matt said, shoving another handful of chips into his mouth. "Hey, Danny, wanna see me finish off these chips while I'm doing a headstand?"

"Don't," Becca said, knowing deep down that Matt was probably joking, but she couldn't help but say something. "You'll choke if you do that."

"You're no fun," Matt said, a small smile creeping up the side of his mouth in a way that told Becca he was never really planning to attempt the headstand. "How am I supposed to get into the circus when you won't even let me practice?"

"The circus will let you in automatically because you're a clown," Becca said, which made everyone burst out laughing.

"Hey, good one," Matt replied, impressed. "I'm rubbing off on you, I see."

"Whatever." Becca rolled her eyes but still smiled.

Despite the strange way they were brought together, Becca found that she was thankful for her new group of friends. It was good to know they all had each other's backs, no matter what.

"Hey," Kylie said suddenly, the smile fading from her face. "Do you guys hear that?"

Everybody fell quiet, and Becca strained to hear what Kylie was talking about. Sure enough, from somewhere far below the treehouse, there came a voice, strained and desperate.

"Guys," the voice said, getting louder. "I'm here. Open up. I said *open up!*"

"That's Miguel," Frankie whispered as they leaned over to open the door on the floor of the treehouse. "He sounds so upset!"

"What's wrong, Miguel?" Matt called down through the opening, just a few seconds before Miguel climbed into the treehouse, collapsing on the floor once the door was closed again and wiping sweat from his forehead with the back of his hand.

"Nacho." Miguel panted, still struggling to catch his

breath. "He . . . he . . . sorry, I ran the entire way here, my legs feel like Jell-O . . ."

"It's okay, Miguel," Kylie said, looking at her friend in concern. "Slow down. Tell us what happened to Nacho."

Becca realized for the first time that Nacho wasn't with Miguel, which was extremely unusual—usually, the snake could be found with Miguel wherever he went. Of all the friends, Miguel was the one who was the most interested in animals, and his pet snake was no exception. Nacho had braved the heart-pounding summer school incident along with the rest of them, and in turn, he had sort of become a part of the group in his own right.

"The Game Master stole him," Miguel finally said, his voice wavering with emotion. "I went outside to take the trash can to the curb. I swear I could have only been gone for a minute, well, maybe three minutes, since I stopped for a snack before going back upstairs . . ." He took a deep breath. "But when I got back to my room, Nacho was gone from his terrarium."

"Maybe he escaped," Becca suggested, but she realized as soon as she said it how unlikely that was. Nacho never hid from Miguel. He loved swirling up his arm or around his neck to hang out. "Or maybe it really was the Game Master."

"It was," Miguel insisted. "I know for sure because there was a note in the tank. Here, I brought it."

The others waited in anticipation while Miguel dug

through his pockets, finally producing a piece of paper that had been folded over several times. "Sorry," Miguel mumbled as he opened the note and spread it over the floor. "It got kind of sweaty from all the running."

Everyone leaned over the note at once, turning their heads and craning their necks in order to read it.

Nap time's over, the note said, the handwriting hauntingly identical to the notes that had been left for them to find in the school two months ago. *It's time for more games, so keep an eye out for your first clue. Are you ready to do whatever it takes to get back what has been lost?*

"This is horrible!" Miguel said, nearing tears again. "Nacho is probably so scared and wondering where I am!"

Matt put his hand on Miguel's shoulder. "Hey," he said gently. "Don't you worry. We're going to find him."

"That's a promise," Becca added, her voice firm. "We've got this, guys. We're going to smoke the Game Master just like we did last time."

Everyone in the group nodded in unison, and just like that, they were back in action, working together in the wonderful way that only they could, determined to do whatever it took to rescue Elephant the hamster and Nacho the snake.

CHAPTER 2

Matt

Matt watched nervously as Kylie scanned the note as though it were a puzzle. Out of the group, Kylie was the one with a knack for solving puzzles. If there was a clue hidden in the note, she'd certainly be the most likely to discover it first.

"If Nacho is being treated the same as Elephant," Frankie said, offering Miguel an encouraging grin, "the only thing you have to worry about is that he might get his picture taken in a hat or something."

"You're right," Miguel said with a nod, taking another deep breath to calm himself. "At least we know they're being cared for well enough until we can find them."

"Still, though," Kylie mumbled under her breath as she

continued to analyze the note. "It's not right. It's pet-napping, and we need to crack this thing."

"Do you see anything in there that could be a potential clue?" Becca asked, crossing her arms as she peered at the note from over Kylie's shoulder.

"I'm not sure," Kylie said. She tucked a length of her jet-black hair behind her ear and chewed on her lower lip, thinking it over. "I guess it's technically possible, but it mostly just looks like a warning that the first clue is on its way. *Keep an eye out* could mean something more specific, or maybe even *nap time's over*, but what? They're too broad to be good clues, and it wouldn't really be the Game Master's style."

Matt stepped back from the rest of the group, pushing his glasses up his nose as he took a moment to think it through on his own. He saw that across the room, Becca appeared to be doing the same thing. Danny walked slowly in a circle around Kylie as she handed the note back to Miguel, who reluctantly shoved it back into his pocket.

"So, what are we supposed to do now?" Miguel asked. "Just sit around and wait? We've been doing that for the last two months with Elephant, and I'm sorry, but I don't trust the Game Master to take care of Nacho for that long."

"Before we didn't have a note like this," Frankie reminded him. "I don't think the Game Master plans on waiting another two months. . . ."

"There has to be something we can do," Miguel said,

lifting his hand to block the view of Danny's camera. "Anything."

"I can make new flyers," Danny offered. He lowered his camera. "Just like the ones I made for Elephant. Maybe we can spread them out even farther this time. Post them outside the neighborhood."

"That's a good start." Becca nodded. "Thanks, Danny."

"Of course." Danny turned back to Miguel. "Hey, would it be cool with you if I filmed a documentary on Nacho's disappearance? The footage could be useful down the road if we need to review anything, and plus, I could submit it to this film program for kids that's happening over winter break."

"For sure," Miguel said. "Anything if it'll help us find Nacho."

"Awesome." Danny raised the camera again with a grin. "I'm going to capture *everything*."

Matt's stomach turned—maybe because he was nervous for Nacho, but maybe because of all those chips he'd inhaled earlier. He took another step back and accidentally bumped into his robot, Ralphie, who he'd totally forgotten was even there. The realization made Matt sad—at one point, he and Ralphie were as inseparable as Miguel and Nacho, but ever since they got summer schooled by the Game Master, Ralphie just hadn't been the same. The Game Master had done something to Ralphie that day, and no matter how hard he tried, Matt hadn't been able to figure it out or fix it. The robot now had a habit of randomly spewing off nonsensical letters and numbers.

"You wanna bring Ralphie along?" Becca was suddenly standing beside Matt, staring at him as though she knew what he was thinking about. "Maybe he'll like helping."

"Sure," Matt said, frowning. "Or maybe he'll break down or start acting weird again."

"Ralphie is still just as cool as the day you put him together," Frankie added, walking over to kneel down and give the robot a gentle pat on the head. The lights of the robot's eyes lit up, and Ralphie raised his arms toward Frankie.

"Blee-blop-bloop," the warped robotic voice whirred, and Matt sighed. "Five, four, three, two, one."

"Come on, Ralphie," Matt said, picking the robot up and shuffling toward the treehouse ladder. "Time to try to find Nacho and Elephant."

They took turns heading down the ladder of Becca's treehouse, which had been deemed their official clubhouse shortly after the summer school incident.

"If we're going to be walking all over the place, I'm gonna need to change my shoes," Frankie said, looking down at their flip-flops and wiggling toes.

"Same," Kylie said. "Should we meet up at the park in an hour?"

"Perfect," Danny answered with a nod. "That'll give me time to go print some flyers."

"Let's do it," Becca said with a gentle clap.

An hour later, Matt arrived at the park on his scooter, Ralphie secured in the harness that he wore on his back. Everybody else was already there, with Danny making the rounds with his video camera, interviewing his friends about Nacho, having everybody talk about their favorite things about the snake. When Matt rolled up, Danny lowered the camera just long enough to pass out thick stacks of the flyers he'd made for Nacho and Elephant.

"Let's make our way to the edge of the neighborhood and then start spreading out from there," Becca said, and the group moved along. Matt trailed in front of them on his scooter, deep in thought about the Game Master.

"Whoever is doing all of this is really sick," he called over his shoulder to his friends. "I still think it could be Vice Principal Pinter. That guy has always hated me."

"Then why didn't he kidnap Ralphie instead of Elephant and Nacho?" Miguel asked. "Also, Vice Principal Pinter hasn't really been acting suspicious since school started. He even came up to us that one day and asked if we were all right after everything, remember?"

"Exactly," Matt said. "Maybe he was trying to get a peek into the state of the group."

"My money is still on Mrs. Richards," Kylie added. "She's the one who's technically in charge of all the supplies Mr. Verdi needed access to in order to help the Game Master execute their plan. Who else could have handed over the keys to the maintenance closet?"

"Keys can be stolen," Becca reminded Kylie. "To be honest, I've started to doubt that it was any of our teachers. Mr. Verdi might know more than he was originally letting on, but we should be open to considering that the Game Master is a kid, just like us."

"What kind of kid is capable of coming up with a plan so complex?" Matt asked with a laugh, but as soon as he asked the question he realized that the idea wasn't so wild. After all, their group alone had shown itself to be capable of some pretty amazing feats. What if the Game Master *was* a kid?

"But why us?" Frankie wondered out loud, shuffling their feet and kicking little rocks across the street as they walked. "There has to be a reason why we were chosen out of everyone else. Before we were summer schooled, none of us really hung out, except for Becca and Matt."

"And that wasn't exactly by choice," Becca said, making Matt laugh. She wasn't wrong. "I'm just hoping that the first clue shows up sooner rather than later."

Before long, the group reached the edge of the neighborhood, and the weight of Ralphie in the harness was causing Matt's back to hurt. "I'm gonna let Ralphie walk around," he announced to nobody in particular, removing the robot from the harness and setting it in a nearby patch of grass. "Maybe he'll be able to help in some way."

"That's the spirit," Danny said, kneeling behind Ralphie to get a good shot with his camera. "Go forth and search, my metal-tastic friend!"

Ralphie replied by toddling clumsily straight ahead, his arms waving around as he took a sudden sharp turn into a tree, which knocked him on his back, his arms and legs pumping like an overturned beetle.

"Whoops," Matt said, rushing forward to help set the robot upright. When he did, Ralphie put his arms down and turned his head straight toward Matt. "Listen," the robot said, the first time it'd spoken something that wasn't complete nonsense in two months. "Listen carefully."

"Did you hear that?" Matt demanded, and Danny nodded excitedly, making sure to come close enough to record everything. The others gathered around also, waiting in anticipation for what might come next.

"Listen carefully," Ralphie the robot repeated, before going off on a ramble of numbers. "N thirty-four, three, thirteen point two eight seven. W one hundred eighteen, fourteen, thirty-three point nine five seven."

"What in the world?" Matt said, confused, but Kylie sprang into action, shushing everybody as she retrieved a small notepad from her pocket. Ralphie repeated the same numbers over and over, Kylie scribbling them in her book furiously.

"Is that an address?" Frankie asked.

"That's too long to be an address," Becca said, peering down at the robot curiously. "But it certainly sounds like something."

"This definitely isn't random," Matt confirmed. "Ralphie's been saying weird stuff ever since summer, but nothing like this. This is different."

"Listen," Ralphie said, then went on to repeat the sequence yet again. Was it possible they'd found their first clue?

"Everybody," Matt said as Danny moved the camera from the robot to everybody's faces one by one, "I think this is the doing of the Game Master."

"The first official clue!" Becca squealed, jumping up in excitement. "Finally! Something we can work with. We're on our way, Miguel."

The group cheered, surrounding Kylie to look at the numbers written in the notepad. Ralphie continued to repeat the sequence, his eyes blinking. Matt felt relieved to know that whatever was going on, the group was sure to figure it out before too long. Maybe they'd even be able to get Nacho and Elephant back by the end of the weekend!

CHAPTER 3

Becca

"So it begins," Becca said, biting her lip as she thought about everything the numbers could possibly mean. Maybe they represented important dates? Or maybe the sequence was in code, something they'd need to find a way to translate into words.

"Something about this is familiar," Kylie said, staring at the sequence of numbers in her notepad. "I swear I'm *this close* to cracking it . . ."

"Maybe the rest of us should split up and hang some flyers while we wait," Becca suggested, the promise of a new clue making her eyes shine. "There's no harm in putting them up before we get started on whatever this code turns out to be."

With new hope putting a skip in everyone's step, the group was able to post the flyers far and wide around the front edge of the neighborhood. Whoever the Game Master was, Becca thought, they had to have friends and family in their life—maybe someone would recognize Elephant and Nacho as someone's recent additions and turn them in. She smiled at the colorful flyer Danny had designed; the word *STOLEN!* was emblazoned across the top in bright-yellow letters outlined in black, and the photos he'd chosen to use of Elephant and Nacho were perfectly adorable.

"You did a great job on these," she called down the street to Danny, who was filming Kylie analyzing the first clue.

Danny flashed her a smile and thumbs-up, apparently not wanting to yell back while he was recording. Becca carefully crossed the street in order to add her last flyer to the bulletin board outside the dog park, then rejoined the group, who were returning to where Kylie and Danny were. Matt rode around on his scooter, Ralphie in the safety of the harness on his back once again.

"Maybe we can see the sequence in a different way," Miguel said, pulling out a piece of sidewalk chalk from the side pocket of his cargo pants. He took a glance over Kylie's shoulder before hurrying to copy the sequence on the sidewalk, running back every few seconds to memorize the next section of numbers.

"What was the second letter, the one starting the second

half of the number chain?" he eventually called back to Kylie, apparently too tired to run back and forth anymore. "Was it a V?"

"W," Kylie called back. "As in . . ." She paused, and her eyes grew wide. "Holy cow, I think I figured it out."

"What?" Miguel answered, not quite understanding. "As in . . . ?"

"West," Kylie said, standing up with her head held high. "This isn't an address per se, but these numbers could very well *lead* us to an address."

"How?" Becca asked, impressed and excited. She knew Kylie could figure it out!

"Have any of you ever heard of DMS?" Kylie walked over to Miguel, took the sidewalk chalk from his hand, and bent down to finish writing out the sequence.

"Erm, no," Frankie admitted, watching Kylie stand and wipe the chalk from her hands on the front of her jeans.

"Me either," Matt said, slowing his scooter to a stop nearby.

Danny didn't answer, too focused on getting everybody else's answers on camera.

"DMS," Becca repeated. "Wait, wait, I think we learned about that during our geography unit."

"Yes we did," Kylie said, nodding excitedly. "Do you remember what it stands for?"

Becca tried to remember what Miss Pritchet had said in class that day, but she could only remember how she'd been secretly drawing a gymnastics comic in the margins of her notebook. "Something about seconds," she said slowly. "Minutes and seconds?"

"Degrees, minutes, seconds," Kylie confirmed, looking over the sequence on the sidewalk once again. "The clue is a geographic coordinate expression. The N in this stands for North. The W stands for West. And the numbers describe the latitude and longitude of . . . somewhere."

"Somewhere?" Miguel repeated. "As in, where we can find Nacho and Elephant?"

"Maybe," Kylie said, pulling out her cell phone. "At the very least, it should lead to the next clue." She motioned for Becca to come join her in looking at the screen, and Becca stepped eagerly forward. "I'm going to plug these coordinates into Google Maps and see if anything pops up."

"You're a genius," Becca breathed. Her heart was racing with excitement. They were able to get this clue figured out way faster than they got their first clue at the school. Already they were working as more of a team from the get-go.

"Well?" Danny asked from behind the lens, stepping dramatically forward to get a close-up of Becca and Kylie. "What does it say?"

Kylie finished entering the coordinates and pushed the *go* button. Almost instantly, a map popped up, complete with a blue teardrop pin that marked their new destination. *3322 Gurley Street,* the address on the sidebar read.

"*The Gurley Street house?*" Becca and Kylie both yelled at the same time, and Becca's heart went from racing because she was excited to racing because she was nervous.

"Wait. What?" Frankie echoed, their voice cracking in disbelief. "Did you just say that the address belongs to the Gurley Street house?"

"Well," Matt said with an empty chuckle. "This just got a whole lot more interesting, didn't it?"

"For the documentary's sake," Danny cut in, moving the camera back and forth between them all in a confused sort of manner. "Remind the audience where exactly Gurley Street is and why everybody's acting this way about it?"

Becca suddenly remembered that Danny's family had only moved to town a few years ago, and it was likely he'd never heard of the Gurley Street house until now. "It's not that far from here, actually," she said, nodding toward the section of streets behind them. "It's in the next neighborhood over from ours."

"Oh, so it's close!" Danny said, breaking out into a smile. "That's great news, right? We can go there right now!"

"No way!" Frankie cried out, raising their hands in fear. "The Gurley Street house is haunted—for real."

"A haunted house?" Danny answered in disbelief. "All this time there's been a *real* haunted house just a hop, skip, and jump away, and none of you have ever mentioned it until now?"

"Because it's creepy." Becca tried to think of the best way to explain the pit of dread that formed in her stomach at the mere mention of the house on Gurley Street. "Growing up, everybody knew about the house. You just didn't play over there. The street is on the back edge of the neighborhood, where the forest begins, and there's only one house on it. It's tucked pretty far back into the trees. It's dark and creepy back there."

"Definitely creepy," Miguel said with a nod. "Definitely haunted."

"'I ain't 'fraid of no ghosts,'" Matt said, solemnly quoting the *Ghostbusters* theme song. "If that's where we're supposed to go next, that's where we're supposed to go."

"But I thought they tore that house down ages ago," Becca said, her voice moving faster and faster as she spoke. "There's no way it's still there, right?"

"Oh, it's there all right." Kylie's eyebrows were knit together. "My older sister and her friends went to look at it last Halloween on a dare."

Becca didn't know what to say. She'd been so excited when Kylie first cracked the clue, and she had hardly been able to wait to see what address the coordinates would pull up. But the house on Gurley Street? Why would the Game Master want them to go there? Was it possible that's where he was keeping Elephant and Nacho? The idea of even *looking* at that house from a distance gave Becca the serious creeps.

She didn't want to look like a wimp in front of Matt and the others, but Becca couldn't deny that she'd been terrified of that house ever since she was a little kid.

"Let's think this through," she suggested, realizing immediately that she was only trying to figure out a way to buy more time. "What exactly did the Game Master mean by sending the address?"

Matt blinked at her for a few seconds. "Um," he said, raising a suspicious brow at Becca's nervous question. "I'm pretty sure they meant for us to *go* there, right?"

"It'd seem that way," Kylie added with a nod. "At least we're all together."

"No way," Frankie said, and Becca let out a sigh of relief that she apparently wasn't the only one feeling hesitation. "There is no way we can go there. Even all together. The place is *haunted*. You heard that part, right? *Haunted!*"

"This just got wild, folks," Danny said, turning the camera around to face himself as he spoke. "The most recent headway in the case reveals that the team will be going to an actual haunted house. Will this documentary end up becoming a horror film?" He let out a dramatic evil laugh that reminded Becca of Dracula or something.

She realized that she'd broken out into a nervous sweat, and also that Matt was watching her carefully. She couldn't let him know how scared she was at the idea of going to the house, but she also felt like hiding underneath the covers of her bed at the mere thought of doing so.

"You okay?" Matt asked. Not mocking or mean, like he might have said it just a year ago, but like he was genuinely concerned about her.

"I'm fine," she insisted, flashing a forced smile for proof. "I'm totally fine."

"I'm not," Frankie said, the color drained from their face. "I sort of feel like I'm going to puke, actually."

Becca wasn't happy that Frankie wasn't feeling well, but she was certainly grateful to have something to shift the focus to. "Uh-oh, that's not good!" she said, her voice higher pitched than she'd hoped for. "We'd better get you something to eat right away. Maybe take a little break until you're feeling better . . ."

"I think some water would help," Frankie said, following Becca's lead back toward their own neighborhood. "We've been out walking for a while now."

"Let's go," Becca called back to the others, who reluctantly followed, Matt looking after her curiously. "We can figure out our next move as soon as Frankie's feeling better."

She tried to carry herself with as much confidence as possible, but as they walked back to the clubhouse, Becca couldn't help but think about what the Game Master might have planned for them at the haunted house on Gurley Street. She wouldn't be able to put off going forever.

Soon, they'd have to go check it out.

CHAPTER 4

Matt

Matt followed Becca back to the clubhouse, weaving in and out between everybody on his scooter.

"Let's stop at my house really quick before heading to Becca's," Frankie suggested, apparently feeling a lot better now that the group wasn't heading straight to the Gurley Street house. "I have some snacks I can throw together for everybody. Can't expect ourselves to be clue-cracking ready until our stomachs are nice and full, right?"

"I'm still not convinced we need to actually *go* to the house," Becca said in a weak voice, turning onto Frankie's street. "There might be something more to it than that."

Matt raised an eyebrow at her. Since when did she play

dumb over stuff like this? Matt knew that Becca was smart enough to realize that being given an address by the Game Master could only mean one thing: they needed to go to there. "What if the Game Master lives in the house?" he asked her, speeding his scooter up until he was riding at her side and able to see her face. "What if that's where he's keeping Elephant and Nacho?"

"That seems more likely than any other option," Kylie said from behind them.

"But nobody lives in that house," Becca said with disgust. "It's totally run down."

After they stopped by Frankie's, who hustled inside to grab a small backpack and fill it with crackers, fruit snacks, and, of course, cheese, the group returned to the clubhouse. Only once they were safely inside Becca's treehouse did she look a little more relaxed.

"Thanks for bringing all this stuff, Frankie," she said as she stacked a piece of cheese on top of a cracker. "I think I was hungrier than I knew."

"Cheese makes everything better," Frankie said with a nod. They held up their own stack, which contained three crackers and four pieces of cheese.

"So, let's recap everything that's happened so far." Danny turned the camera on himself again, looking thoughtfully into the distance as he tapped his chin with his finger. "Two months ago, the crew escaped the maniacal clutches of the illusive Game Master, only to discover that Angel's hamster, Elephant, had been hamster-napped. Now Miguel's left-hand man—er, snake—has also been taken. The Game Master left the crew a code through Matt's robot, Ralphie, who may or may not have been hacked."

Matt's stomach dropped at the idea of Ralphie being hacked. As cool as it was for Ralphie to have been the one to help the friends discover the clue, Matt worried about what else might happen to his beloved robot before all of this was said and done. Would Ralphie ever return to his regular state? Maybe if they beat the Game Master again, whoever it was would be willing to tell Matt how to fix Ralphie. More than anything, Matt missed the robotic buddy he'd worked so hard to build. He hoped the group was able to beat this game, and fast.

"Now," Danny continued, "we've been left with nothing but an address. Where is the address located, you ask? A haunted house that has been terrifying local children for years. The house"—he paused dramatically, waggling his eyebrows at the camera—"on Guuurley Streeeet!"

"Cut it out, Danny," Becca said through a mouthful of cheese and crackers. "When you see it, you'll understand why nobody wanted to go there."

"For the record, I am down to go," Kylie said with a shrug.

"Same," Miguel said. "I don't get why we're wasting time when we could be on our way to save Nacho and Elephant!"

"You said, 'when you see it,'" Matt said to Becca, challenging her. "Does that mean you're finally ready to admit that we need to go over there?"

"I don't know," Becca said, still sounding unsure. "Maybe we should wait until tomorrow. You know, bright and early and all that."

"That'd be a colossal waste of time," Kylie said, growing impatient. "It's still early. There's plenty of day left. Plus, I have plans tomorrow."

"We need to go today," Miguel agreed. "No ifs, ands, or buts, Becca. Nacho needs me."

Becca swallowed hard, and Frankie looked like they might be feeling sick again.

"Look," Matt said gently. "If you guys are too scared, you don't have to come."

He'd meant for it to make her feel better, but instead, Becca's face flushed to the color of a tomato. "I'm not scared!" she insisted, her voice coming out like a squeak.

"I am," Frankie said. "I'm not too tough to admit it."

"To be clear, I'm scared too," Miguel said. "But I don't have as much of a choice. These are my and my little brother's pets. We love them too much for me to let fear get in the way. Look, we all survived last time, didn't we?"

Even Frankie had to nod.

"Then we'll get through this game just like we got through the last one," Miguel went on, standing up to brush the cracker crumbs from his shirt. "Who's with me? Who's ready to go to the house on Gurley Street?"

"I am," Kylie answered immediately, standing to join Miguel. "Let's do this thing."

"You know I'm there," Danny said, shuffling over to join the other two. "I bet I'm gonna get some real wicked footage throughout the course of this. Bring it on, Game Master."

Matt smiled and joined the group. "Of course I'm in," he said, turning to Becca, who was still sitting beside Frankie, biting her lip nervously. "What about you, Becks?"

Becca's eyes widened in disbelief. "You mean to say you're all going to go, whether we join you or not? You'd actually leave us behind?"

"I'm sorry, Becca," Miguel said, standing his ground. "But yes. We'd like to have you with us, of course, but I'm just not okay with sitting on this a minute longer. Pets' lives may be at stake."

Becca and Frankie considered it, meeting each other's eyes in silence. As if communicating in some unspoken language, Becca raised her eyebrow just the slightest bit, and Frankie responded with a nod.

"Fine," Becca said. "We'll do it."

"Yes!" Kylie and Miguel cheered, rushing forward to exchange high fives with Becca and Frankie. Danny got the whole scene on tape, of course. Matt thought that it'd make for a great moment in the documentary.

"One crew, coming together once again for round two," Danny narrated, moving the camera excitedly over the group.

"Okay," Becca said with one last sigh, then stood up straight and clapped her hands together. "If we're really gonna do this, we need to go prepared. Not like last time. We have to do whatever we can to stay a few steps ahead of the Game Master."

"Agreed." Matt nodded. "We need to gear up somehow."

"We'll need flashlights," Becca said. "I can't imagine that we'd regret having extra light sources handy."

"And I'll make sure to bring some extra batteries for my camera," Danny said. "Don't want to risk running out and missing anything that might help us later on during a rewatch. I'll grab my motion detector, too."

"I can bring a few pairs of binoculars, just in case," Frankie added, and Matt couldn't help but feel proud of them. Not a lot of kids would be brave enough to put aside their fears in order to help a friend. That's what made their group special, Matt knew. He felt lucky to be a part of it.

"You gonna bring Ralphie, Matt?" Miguel asked. "Maybe he'll end up helping us out with some more clues."

Matt thought about it for a minute, looking at the robot that he'd set in the corner of the treehouse, the power switch turned off. "I think I'm going to leave him here, actually," he said, surprising even himself with his answer. Usually, he took Ralphie with him *everywhere*. "I don't want to risk anything else happening to him. I need to make sure he stays safe."

"That's totally understandable," Becca said. "I wouldn't put it past the Game Master to try to steal Ralphie too, on top of everything else."

"Exactly," Matt said. "It'll be best to have Ralphie sit this one out."

The rest of the group nodded in understanding.

"Um." Miguel shifted his weight from one foot to the other. "I want to say thank you for agreeing to help me find Elephant and Nacho. I don't know what I'd do without you all."

"Hey," Becca said with a smile. "That's what friends are for, yeah? We're all in this together. The Game Master has made sure of that."

"This darn Game Master," Kylie said. "I sure can't wait to find out who they are."

"Maybe we'll find out this time," Matt suggested. "We almost caught them last time, and we were a lot less prepared than we are now."

"Okay, team," Becca said, and Matt could tell she was feeling a lot better about everything than she had before. Frankie too. "Let's get to packing up for the journey. Flashlights, extra batteries, whatever you think might be helpful to us. I'll make sure to grab some water bottles, too. Gotta stay hydrated!"

The group started going down the ladder of the treehouse one by one. Matt purposefully went last, to get one last moment with Ralphie before he left.

"See you soon, buddy," he said. "Sorry I have to leave you behind this time."

He went down the ladder and joined Becca in searching through her garage for any final supplies that might be useful. They packed up a small leather backpack of Becca's from a school hiking trip they took last year, eventually meeting up with the others in the yard once again. Everybody looked ready to take on the Game Master.

"Alrighty," Becca said after assessing what everybody else brought in their own packs. "Everyone ready to play the game?"

"Ready," they echoed, Miguel the loudest of all.

"Okay, then," Becca said, taking the first move to lead the crew out. "Let's go."

CHAPTER 5

Becca

You can do this, Becca told herself, believing it in her heart as she led the group down the street. *No doubt.*

"So tell me more," Danny said, walking at the end of the group so he could get everybody in the shot. "Tell the audience about what you've heard and seen at this infamous Gurley Street house."

"Supposedly there's a man named Mr. O'Hallahan who lives there," Kylie replied.

"Nobody's ever seen him, though," Becca added. She thought about the first time she ever saw the house as a kid: while trick-or-treating with her family. "That's why I think he's a myth."

"Well, somebody has to have lived there," Miguel said. "At one point or another."

"Do you mean to hint that the house might be occupied by Mr. O'Hallahan's *ghost*?" Danny asked for effect. "The plot thickens."

"I saw a shadow in the window once," Matt said as he hopped his scooter from the sidewalk to the street. "For real. It was in the middle of the day, too, so I know it wasn't just my eyes playing tricks on me."

Becca tried to remember if she'd ever heard of anybody who had actually seen or met Mr. O'Hallahan—she couldn't. "Why would the Game Master have us go to the house if there was someone living inside?"

"Maybe the Game Master forced him to participate in the game, just like with Mr. Verdi during summer school," Frankie offered. "Or maybe they know that the house is abandoned."

"Maybe the Game Master *is* Mr. O'Hallahan," Danny threw out, to a chorus of groans.

"That would make less than no sense," Miguel said. "Why would someone we've never met decide to build an elaborate game just for us?"

"True," Danny admitted. "To be honest, I just thought it'd make a great twist."

Becca had to smile at that. It sounded like something straight out of *Scooby-Doo*. She imagined Danny filming the group as they dramatically removed the mask off someone who was dressed like a ghost, only to reveal some old man with a serious boredom problem.

"So nobody here has ever gone inside?" Danny asked. "Have you even gotten close enough to peek through the windows?"

"No way!" The rest of the group cried out together.

"So for all you know there could be a sweet little old lady living inside with her cat," Danny scoffed. "And the house could be perfectly cozy and welcoming."

"Yeah right," Matt said with a laugh. "We'll see how you feel once you actually see it for yourself."

Before she knew it, Becca was crossing the street to pass over to the neighboring development of houses. "We're getting closer," Kylie said as they all looked at the trees. "I don't think I've been back here in years."

"Me either," Miguel admitted. "Nobody ever wanted to play back here. Even the kids who lived close by."

"One time my dog Radish escaped out of our yard," Kylie said, her voice getting low. "My sister and I had to chase him all the way back here. He went through the trees, but luckily we were able to get him before he ran into Mr. O'Hallahan's yard."

"That would have been terrifying," Matt said from his scooter. "Imagine if Radish had gone inside!"

"I wonder if the Game Master is going to try to make us go inside," Becca wondered. "I'm not sure I'm up for that."

"Either way," Frankie said, "the entire forest around that house is spooky."

The trees got closer and closer as they approached the end of the street.

"I wonder what my mom is making for dinner tonight," Matt blurted randomly, and that's when Becca realized that he was just as nervous as she was, he'd just been doing a better job of hiding it. She tried to remind herself that Elephant and Nacho needed their help, and that when her nana's zoetrope had been stolen during the summer school game, the entire group had come together to help her get it back.

"We're almost there," Kylie announced, and Danny let out a whoop of excitement.

The closer they got to Gurley Street, the less everybody wanted to talk. Even Danny put his camera down for the last bit, saying that he'd start filming again when they were approaching the house. Becca's imagination ran wild with all the potential things the Game Master might put them through. She wondered if the Game Master was inside the house waiting for them right that very moment. She wondered if Elephant was still in the tiny clown costume that he'd been wearing in the last photograph the Game Master had sent them.

When they reached the corner sign that read Gurley Street, Danny turned his camera on again, making sure to get a good shot of the sign, as well as everybody walking past it toward the end of the street.

"You guys weren't kidding before," he commented as they made their way down the quiet, shady street. "There aren't any other houses on this entire street. I can't even see the house. It's like the road just disappears into the forest. Like the forest is a giant mouth."

"See?" Kylie said, raising a brow at Danny with a grin. "We told you it's freaky—and you haven't even seen the house itself yet."

As they got farther away from any houses and closer to the trees, Becca's palms started sweating. As they entered the forest, it got noticeably darker, as though the sun weren't welcome. The air felt thicker somehow, which Becca knew sounded ridiculous, but it really did feel different than the light, sunny air out on the street. The air took on a bitter chill, and Becca shivered, zipping up her hoodie to try to escape it. She considered getting out one of the water bottles and taking a sip, but she realized it'd be smarter to save the water for later in case they really needed it.

"Did you hear that?" Frankie asked suddenly, stopping in their tracks to peer through the trees to their right. "It sounded like a twig snapping."

"It was probably an animal," Becca asserted, making herself believe that it was true so she didn't turn around and run screaming. "Lots of squirrels and rabbits and stuff around here, I'd imagine."

"Definitely a squirrel," Kylie said, although she didn't sound too sure. "Let's keep moving."

Before long, the group was able to see the beginnings of the outline of the house, tall and looming in the shadows of the forest. Becca's mouth opened a little bit at the sight; she'd forgotten just how huge the house was. It was closer to a mansion, really.

Surrounding the house was a wide stretch of uneven fencing, the yard within overgrown and dense. A mailbox was posted directly in front of the fence, looking weirdly out of place. Inside the fence was a particularly large and old-looking tree.

"Holy moly," Danny said under his breath, stopping to get his first shot of the house. "I feel cold inside just *looking* at it."

"See?" Frankie said, crossing their arms and looking ahead without blinking. "It really is something, right?"

It sure was. Becca noticed the paint peeling from the walls and how the shutters made the windows look like droopy eyes watching them all, daring them to come closer. There weren't any birds singing near the house, and if there were indeed squirrels in the forest, they didn't seem to want to come too close. From all appearances, the house was totally empty. There was no car parked in front, and no lights shone through the dark, large windows.

"So what do we do now?" Matt asked. "The Game Master didn't provide us with anything except the location."

"I suppose we should do a sweep of the yard to see if there are any clues around," Becca said, trying to stand firm in her position as the leader of the pack. If she acted like she wasn't nervous, maybe it'd help everybody else to feel less nervous themselves. "We can split up into three groups of two so nobody is alone."

"Great idea," Danny said, following Miguel to the gate. "We'll check out this front half of the yard."

"Me and Frankie can check out the sides," Kylie volunteered, and the two linked arms and went off.

"I guess that leaves you and me to explore the back," Matt said to Becca with a nervous chuckle. "How'd we get stuck with the spookiest part?"

"Maybe the back of the house is less creepy than the front," Becca tried, which put a smile on Matt's face. "Unlikely, I know, but let's go for it."

"After you, Becks," he said, abandoning his scooter by the mailbox.

The sound of dead leaves crunching beneath their sneakers chilled Becca's bones a little bit. This house was straight out of a scary movie. Hopefully there were no monsters or chainsaw-wielding madmen lurking in any of these shadows.

Don't be ridiculous, she told herself. *You're letting your imagination get too carried away.*

"I wonder if the Game Master is watching us right now," Matt whispered, which didn't help things one bit.

"If they are, I hope they see this," Becca said, breaking out into the silliest dance she could think of. Matt's eyes widened in surprise as he took in the sight of her before he burst out laughing. Becca was glad—they needed to lighten the mood around here a bit. She was just glad that Danny's camera hadn't been close enough to see it.

"I'm going to need you to do that every time stuff gets too spooky around here," Matt said, wiping his eyes as he stopped laughing. "That was the greatest thing I've seen in a long time."

"We'll see," she said, out of breath but still smiling.

When they made their way around the back of the house, Becca was both relieved and disappointed to see that there wasn't anything out of the ordinary in sight. She turned toward Matt to ask him if he wanted to go back when the sound of Frankie's yells stopped her.

"I found something!" Frankie was crying out. "Everybody come here!"

They found Frankie and the others gathered around the mailbox. There, stuck to the back of it, was a familiar green, backlit GM sticker.

The Game Master symbol!

CHAPTER 6

Matt

With an excited gasp, Matt opened the mailbox and peered inside. "Whoa," he said, reaching his hand into the dark cubby as the others watched. He winced as he felt around the mailbox, hoping that there weren't any creepy crawlies hidden inside. "There's something in here."

"What is it?" Becca asked, and Miguel bounced up and down on his toes.

"There are a few things."

First, Matt pulled out a small velvet bag that was a beautiful jewel-toned purple, which seemed weirdly out of place in its dark and dreary surroundings. Then he pulled out an envelope with another GM sticker sealing it shut. Becca plucked the letter from Matt's hand as he opened the purple velvet bag to see what was inside.

"There's a bunch of little plastic pieces," he said, pulling one out to inspect it closer. It looked like a little board game tile, like the kind you'd see in Scrabble. On one side of the tile there were tiny paw prints in a line, and on the other, the letter E.

"Those look like hamster prints," Miguel said when he saw the paw prints on the other side of the tile. Matt reached in for another tile to see if they were all the same, but one had the letter H on one side and strange swirly lines on the other.

"And those look like snake prints!" Miguel cried, grabbing the tile to take a closer look. "One step closer to Elephant and Nacho."

"What does the letter say, Becca?" Kylie asked. Matt noticed that Becca had removed a piece of paper from the envelope and was reading it silently to herself. She lowered the paper to show that it contained a letter written with glued-on magazine letter clippings.

"Why'd they have to use the magazine letters like that?" Frankie said with a shiver. "That is so creepy."

"They wanted to hide their handwriting," Kylie theorized, but then Frankie pointed out that the Game Master could have just printed out a typed letter like all the other times.

"It was meant to unsettle us," Frankie insisted, biting their lip. "I just know it."

"*Welcome to the house on Gurley Street,*" Matt read out loud from the letter in Becca's hands. "*Your first task is to decode the message hidden within these tiles. You might want to hurry, though; I'm not so sure this place would be safe after nightfall. If you want to save the hamster and the snake, you'll have to work together to beat the game I've created just for you. Have fun, and make sure not to wander off alone into any dark corners—you never know what might be waiting for you in the shadows.*"

The letter was signed *THE GAME MASTER*.

"Holy fruits," Frankie said. They wrapped their arms around themselves. "I knew this would be some spooky stuff, but this is really getting to be next level."

"How many tiles are in the bag?" Kylie demanded, swiftly snapping into action. "You heard what the Game Master said. I have no intention of being here past dark."

"Same," Becca agreed, and Miguel looked nervously at the house.

"There's a lot of tiles," Matt answered Kylie. He looked around for any flat surface large enough to sort the tiles on, his eyes finding nothing until they landed on the wide wooden porch of the house. "Let's do it over here."

The group made their way to the porch, then they sat around the pile of dumped-out tiles in a circle. "Where do we even begin?" Matt said, looking hopelessly to the scattered pile of letters, hamster prints, and snake prints. "This looks really complicated."

"Not if I have anything to say about it," Kylie murmured, already going to work by sorting the tiles into separate piles according to letter and print pattern. "There has to be a way to figure this out or the Game Master wouldn't have given it to us."

"That's true," Becca said. "It's almost like the Game Master *wants* us to beat their game, they just don't want to make it easy. We can do this if we put our heads together."

"So obviously the tiles are going to end up spelling out a message," Miguel noted. "But the question is how to figure out what order to arrange them in? There must be a pattern."

"Exactly," Kylie said. Her eyes darted back and forth between the separated piles. "If there's an order, I'd imagine it has something to do with the animal prints. One of them, either the hamster print or snake print, must be an indication of the start of each word. But which one would be more likely to come first?"

"The hamster prints," Frankie said, nodding. "It has to be, because Elephant was stolen first!"

"The word *hamster* also comes before the word *snake*, alphabetically speaking," Kylie agreed, nodding as she leaned forward to scoop away all the hamster-print tiles. "I'd say that's as solid of a start as any."

Kylie lined up all the hamster-print tiles in a row, flipping them over to reveal the letters they held. "If our theory is correct, these tiles are going to start every word in the message," she said. "That would mean there are fifteen words total."

"Nice," Matt said, looking over his shoulder to the empty window behind them. "This is moving along already."

In the distance, the wind blew through the trees, making it sound like the forest was full of whispers. The sooner they could beat the game and get out of here, the better.

"Now we need to use the snake-print tiles to try to create words on them," Kylie continued. "After we've made fifteen words using every spare tile, we'll be able to try to rearrange them into any sort of message that makes sense or reads like a clue."

"All right," Danny said, speaking for the first time since Matt opened the mailbox. "I think I might be able to help with this. I'm really good at spelling, and if there are multiple ways to create one word, I can get them all on film in case we need to look back. We should be able to move through the code pretty quickly that way."

"Perfect," Kylie said. She scooted over to make an extra space so Danny could move over and work beside her. "Let's get to work, then."

As much as Matt hoped that they would effortlessly build the words and figure out the message, it turned out to be easier said than done. For example, one of the hamster-print tiles showed an A—did that mean that they should consider words that started with A using letters from the snake-print pile, or did the message simply have the letter A in it somewhere? Luckily, there was only one hamster-print tile with an A, so Kylie suggested they skip trying to build on the A until there were fewer tiles to work with.

"I can't help but notice there are two E's and one N in the hamster-print tiles," Becca noted as Danny tried to help Kylie build a word on an H tile and film at the same time. "Do you think it's reasonable to assume that the E tiles are for Elephant, and the N tile is for Nacho?"

"Let's see if the snake-print pile has what we'd need to build those words," Kylie said, apparently relieved to have some level of direction for a solid start.

To the group's excitement, there were indeed the tiles necessary to spell both *Elephant* and *Nacho*, which left them with way fewer tiles and a task that was far less overwhelming to tackle. After the big break, everybody felt more confident trying to build words with what was left, and before Matt knew it, they had a full list of fifteen words and zero spare tiles left.

"We're getting closer!" Kylie said with a grin, and Becca clapped her hands together in joy.

"Now we just need to find out which order these words go in," Frankie noted.

Everybody else started throwing out suggestions, but Matt blocked everything out and stared at the list of words, trying to work out potential answers without being influenced by the other suggestions:

THEM

NACHO

FUN

FIND

HAVE

AND

I

ELEPHANT

HAVE

SOME

TO

ENTER

AND

HOUSE

THE

"The word *have* appears twice," Matt mumbled, and nobody heard him except Becca.

"Yeah?" she asked encouragingly, apparently recognizing that he was on to something.

"*I have Elephant and Nacho,*" he said, and Becca hushed the others so they'd listen to Matt.

Kylie took the words aside and arranged them in the order Matt had suggested. Looking at the words that were left over, she was able to push the message a little bit further. "*To find them . . .*"

"*Enter the house . . .*," Frankie continued, reaching forward to grab the appropriate tiles to build after Matt and Kylie's bits.

"*And have some fun*," Miguel finished. Danny stood with his camera to get the entire message in the shot, reading the final form out loud.

"*I have Elephant and Nacho. To find them, enter the house and have some fun.*"

"We did it!" Kylie cheered, and everybody stood up and exchanged high fives.

"Great job," Becca said. "We couldn't have done it without everybody's help. I bet you anything the Game Master didn't expect us to crack that one so quickly."

"But now we have to go inside," Kylie said, looking nervously to the front door of the house. "If we want to see what the next puzzle is and keep this crazy game going."

"Are we seriously going to just . . . obey whatever the Game Master tells us to do?" Frankie asked. "I can't help but feel like it's a bad idea to just waltz on in there. . . ."

"We have to," Miguel reminded them. "Elephant and Nacho are in there somewhere. The only way to figure it out is to follow the clues all together."

"Wait," Becca said, a mischievous grin blooming on her face. "What if we pulled one over on the Game Master?"

CHAPTER 7

Becca

"We should split up," Becca suggested, which caused the group to cast doubtful stares. Kylie twirled her hair around her finger with a confused expression, and Matt raised an eyebrow at Becca.

"Are you kidding?" Frankie said. "That's like, rule number one in a horror movie. *Don't split up!* Why would we do that, especially when the Game Master clearly wants us to stick together?"

"But that's exactly why," Becca explained. "The Game Master wouldn't expect for us to split up to search for Elephant and Nacho. Maybe if we do, we'll end up covering more ground and finding the animals sooner."

The group was quiet as they thought it over. Becca could tell she almost had them convinced—nobody wanted to spend any more time here than absolutely necessary, and this would be a way to potentially cut the game in half.

"Look," she said a little more gently. "We know the game, and we know how tricky the Game Master can be. Think about it—last time we came so close to catching them! We are capable of beating the game *and* figuring out who the Game Master is. We can do it! Divide and conquer!"

She was met with little nods, and Becca could tell her friends were finally starting to understand what she was trying to say. "All right, Becca," Frankie said with a sigh after the silence. "Who should go with who? And who should do what?"

"Me, you, and Danny can go into the house, like the Game Master said to," Becca answered, and at the sound of his name, Danny moved over to stand between Becca and the door to the creepy old house, his camera ready to capture everything. "Matt, Kylie, and Miguel—you should go around to the backyard and check it out. Matt and I hardly got to look around back there before we heard Frankie calling at the mailbox. Maybe there's something out there that'll reveal a clue about the Game Master or where they're hiding Elephant and Nacho."

"Roger that," Kylie confirmed with a nod, and Matt and Miguel started making their way down the porch steps.

"We'll catch up with you when we can."

"Let us know if you find anything," Miguel called to Becca as they disappeared around the corner.

"Be careful," Matt told them, and Becca nodded and offered a thumbs-up in promise.

"Okay," Becca said after the second group was out of sight, turning back toward Frankie and Danny. "Are you ready?"

"I can't believe I'm about to see the inside of a haunted house," Frankie said, wonder in their voice. "It's like a nightmare, but I can't help but be a little curious. Haven't you always wondered what was in here?"

Becca thought back to the cold, terrible feeling she'd always gotten whenever she walked past Gurley Street or thought about the house. "Yes," she said with a gulp. "Why couldn't the Game Master have chosen, like, a candy store?"

"That'd be pretty . . . *sweet*," Danny said from the behind the camera with a little laugh. "Pun intended."

That made Becca and Frankie smile a little bit. "Let's do this if we're gonna do it," Frankie said, and then turned to wrap their hand around the doorknob. With a twist and a push, the front door swung open, creaking and groaning as it went.

"This is it," Becca said, stepping between Frankie and Danny. "Let's go in at the same time. On the count of three."

"One," Frankie said, taking a deep breath.

"Two," added Danny, who eagerly turned on the light mounted on the front of his camera.

"Three!" they all cried together, and stepped into the shadows of the old house.

It took a second for Becca's eyes to adjust to the darkness. At first, she considered running her hands along the wall to look for a light switch, but she quickly stopped when she saw that the wall was covered in dust and peeling wallpaper.

"Whoa," Frankie said under their breath. "This is wild."

Becca had to agree. Danny filmed her as she looked over the dust-covered furniture and the spiderwebs in every corner. Her eyes stopped as they fell upon the large, dark-red stains all over the carpet. "What is that?" she said, pointing, her stomach turning. "That can't be . . . blood, can it?"

"It's unlikely," Frankie said, their voice shaking. "No way it's blood. There are all sorts of things that could turn this color after a long time."

"I'm gonna go ahead and go with that," Danny added, still kneeling down and zooming in to get a wide, slow, dramatic shot of the stains. "Otherwise I might have to run away screaming."

Becca looked around the rest of the room. It was so dark in here, it almost looked like there were shadows climbing the walls. Thank goodness for the light on Danny's camera, as well as for the sunlight that was able to filter through the filthy, dust-streaked windows.

"The sooner we can get out of here, the better," Becca said. "I think we can all agree on that."

"Absolutely," Frankie and Danny said together.

"Let's spread out a little and check for clues," Becca suggested. "But everybody stay in the same room. We should make sure not to lose sight of each other."

"Agreed." Danny started exploring the area behind the stains, using the light on his camera to light up the darker corners of the room. Frankie moved to the wall right next to the door, looking over the framed photos that hung over the peeling, rotting walls.

Becca walked across the room, stepping carefully around a filthy couch and a cracked coffee table, until she found a dresser of some sort up against a wall. On top of the dresser were a variety of dust-covered trinkets—porcelain cats, miniature teacups, a tiny gold violin with a diamond in the center. "Whoa," she whispered. "Some of this stuff is actually pretty cool."

Beneath the trinkets was a length of lace doily, which had probably been white at one point in time but was now yellow and brown from various stains and gatherings of dirt. She wondered how long the house had been abandoned—clearly nobody could *live* here in the house's current condition.

Right?

"Hey," Danny called from the other side of the room. "You might want to come see this."

"Did you find a clue?" Frankie asked without turning away from the framed portraits on the wall, too entranced by whatever was in the photo.

"Absolutely and definitely," Danny confirmed, which got everyone's attention quick. "Come see what's written on this mirror."

A message on a mirror? Becca quickly made her way over to Danny, who was still filming the mirror that was propped in the back corner of the room. She wasn't able to see the message until she got closer: a question written in shaky, red letters.

What is Danny Watson afraid of?

"I really do not like this," Danny said, and Becca could hear that he was scared. "Remember how last time the Game Master designed puzzles for everyone in the group individually? Well, apparently mine is first this time."

"Oh great," Frankie said with a frown. They crossed their arms over their chest and chewed their lip while they stared at the message. "Well, what's the answer, Danny? Whatever it is might help us move forward in the game right away."

"I don't want to say it," Danny said with a shiver, lowering the camera in a rare moment of discomfort. "Because I can tell you right now, the answer is something that is surrounding us right this very minute. As long as we're in this house, they're around us."

"What?" Becca looked around frantically, hoping to see

something that might offer any insight. "Filth? Creepy pho-tos?"

"Spiders," Danny whispered, turning the camera to his own face. "Have you seen how many spiderwebs there are in here? They're probably everywhere right now. On the carpet. Crawling inside the walls. Nesting in the furniture. This place is like a spider haven!" He flipped the camera around and zoomed up on the various webs that were clustered in the corners of the ceiling to show the proof.

"Creepy crawlies everywhere," Danny said, turning back toward Becca. "What are we supposed to do with that information?"

"I'm not sure," Becca admitted, furrowing her brows as she thought it over. "Last time, the Game Master left lists for us to find. I wonder if maybe there's something hidden in one of the webs?"

"Heck no," Danny said, nodding very firmly back and forth. "There is no way I'm sticking my hand into a *spiderweb*."

"Yeah, I'm gonna go ahead and pass on that too," Frankie said, looking more and more like they wanted to bolt from the house. "I'm not so sure I can do this, Becca."

Becca had to admit that her desire to stick her hand into some dark, creepy spiderweb was less than zero. "I'm not wild about this either," she said, and the friends huddled closer together, looking around. "We just need to find Elephant and Nacho and get out of here."

Right as she finished the sentence, the still-open front door swung closed with a loud boom. Dust rained over them from the ceiling, and the trinkets on the dresser Becca had inspected before rattled in place. Frankie nearly jumped out of their skin, and Becca couldn't help but release a startled yelp.

"How did the Game Master make the door close like that?" Danny demanded, looking around for any evidence of ropes or a pulley system that might explain what had happened. When he found none, everybody rushed over to the entrance, ready to retreat to the safety of the sunlit outside to figure out their next move.

"The wind wasn't strong enough to do that," Frankie said as they approached the door. "Not even close. Something closed that door!"

Becca reached for the doorknob, frantically jiggling it back and forth in an attempt to open the door. "No way," she said, her voice escalating in panic as she tried. How was this possible? She tried again and again, but each time the knob refused to turn. "It's locked!"

CHAPTER 8

Matt

The backyard was a lot larger than Matt had originally noticed when he'd been back with Becca earlier. There was the initial stretch of dirt behind the back porch that he saw the first time, but now he could see that farther behind it, stretching into the forest, was a large patch of overgrown weeds.

"This yard is huge," Kylie remarked, looking over it slowly. "It'll take us a hot minute to sweep through it."

"I hope Elephant and Nacho aren't out here," Miguel said, worry lacing his voice. "Who knows what sorts of predatory animals might have made their home in those weeds?"

"Don't worry," Matt told Miguel. "And don't forget that

all the photos of Elephant that we received from the Game Master showed him totally safe. I doubt the Game Master would want for either of them to get hurt."

"Yeah, you're right." Miguel took a deep breath. "I just can't wait for this to all be over with."

"You and me both," Kylie said dryly, leading the group over to where the weeds reached as high as their heads. "Look, there's some sort of trail that goes into the weeds! Like someone made a path to walk through."

"The Game Master," Matt said under his breath, and Miguel nodded in agreement. One by one, the friends stepped on to the trail in a single-file line, Kylie at the lead, Miguel in the middle, and Matt in the back.

The path snaked around the yard, turning this way and that without much evidence of reason or order. Eventually, they found themselves completely surrounded by weeds that they couldn't see over, and the path split off in two opposite directions.

"You know what?" Kylie said as they stared at the wider trail, trying to see which way they were supposed to go. "This reminds me an awful lot of a labyrinth."

"A labyrinth?" Matt said, straining to remember what the word meant. He remembered, vaguely, a movie his mom had shown him when he was little that featured puppets and a lost girl looking for her baby brother who'd been kidnapped by goblins. "Like a maze?"

"Exactly," Kylie said. "This is a maze. Regardless of which way we go, we need to stick together. Getting separated at this point could be catastrophic."

"You won't see *me* wandering off," Miguel said with a shiver. "This is giving me the creeps. I can't even see the house anymore."

Surprised, Matt turned to see if that was true, and it was. No matter which direction he looked, he couldn't see any sign of the house or the big tree in the front—the weeds were too high.

"Let's try the left turn first," Kylie said, clearly nervous as she looked right one last time. "If we hit a dead end, we'll make our way back here and try the other side. The trick to this is going to be to keep our heads on straight. Try to remember where we have or haven't gone. It'll be hard because everything is going to look the same in these weeds."

"Okay," Matt said, suddenly wishing that he'd been in the group that had gone inside the house. His group had gotten to stay outside, sure, but the darkness of the forest combined with the tall weeds made him feel like the yard was swallowing them whole.

Kylie led them down the left path, which eventually made another few turns before splitting off into yet another choice of direction. "We went left the first time," she said, looking around. "So maybe this time we could go right."

"Left, then right," Matt repeated, trying to memorize the

order in his head. "So if we were going to turn around, we'd want to go right, then left?"

"It'd still be left, then right," Kylie said as they made their way even deeper into the maze. "Because even though we'd want to take opposite turns, we'd have to make them backward."

Already Matt's brain hurt trying to keep track of exactly where they were. By the look on Miguel's face, his did too. Thank goodness they had Kylie with them.

After a few more turns, Kylie stopped and looked around. "Dang it," she said, looking between another set of turns. "I have to be honest right now—I have no idea where we are. Like, are we going in circles? Or does the maze really go this deep?"

"It has to be circles," Matt said, the sight of a nervous Kylie causing a hard pit of dread to form in his stomach. "It feels like we've been walking for a long time."

"I don't think we're going in circles," Miguel said. "The weeds have gotten a little taller, if anything. They weren't this tall before, were they?"

"I don't know," Kylie said, her breath quickening, and Matt could see that she was starting to panic a little bit. "It's like no matter where I look, I feel lost."

Right when it looked like she was about to lose it, something caught Matt's eye on the path ahead. Something bright green on the ground, standing out among the many shades of brown of the weeds.

"Look!" he cried out, pointing to the mark. They all rushed over, Kylie letting out a huge sigh of relief at the sight of it. There, spray painted on the ground, was a neon-green circle, small but noticeable.

"Okay, so we definitely didn't see this before," Kylie said, looking ahead down the path with the circle. "Oh look, there's another circle down there! I think we need to just follow the dots at this point. Thank goodness. I was really starting to freak out there."

The friends eagerly followed the dots on the ground, which eventually lead them to a larger clearing in the weeds, shaped like a big square. For the first time in a long time they were able to stand as a group instead of in a straight line, and Matt felt like he could breathe again, even if only in this enclosed space. In the center of the clearing there was a treasure box.

"Yes!" Kylie cried out, rushing over to the treasure box with the others. "This must mean that we beat the labyrinth!"

"What's inside?" Miguel asked as Kylie fumbled to open it. "Another clue, maybe? The location of Elephant and Nacho?"

The box clicked open to reveal three pieces of folded paper, labeled *One, Two,* and *Three.* With shaking hands, Kylie opened the paper that

was labeled *One*. Inside there was a strange, grid-like sketch, showing lines and rows and boxes. Matt's heart skipped a beat when he noticed the red writing that dominated the top of the paper:

What is Kylie Dao afraid of?

"It's a map," Kylie whispered. "A map of the labyrinth, I think."

"A map is a good thing, right?" Miguel asked, confused. "Why is it asking what you're afraid of?"

"Because there's only one thing in this world I'm afraid of," Kylie admitted, her voice much smaller than it usually was. "Getting lost."

Matt remembered the suffocating feeling of winding through the narrow paths of the maze until they found the clearing with the treasure box. He remembered how panicked Kylie had started to become when they thought that they might be getting lost.

"We're going to get out of here," Matt told Kylie, leaning down to put his hand on her shoulder. "I promise. And if all else fails, we can always scream until the others hear us. We could follow their voices to get out of here."

"You're right." Kylie stood up with purpose, her posture strong, and opened the other two pieces of paper to check them before doing anything else. They were both identical copies of the first map, but each one had a different potential escape route traced in different colors. The first map's escape route was outlined in blue, the second one was red, and the third was green.

"One of these is the real way to escape," Kylie said, looking between them. "The other two are fakes."

"So how are we supposed to know which is which?" Miguel asked. "If we choose one of the wrong ones first, wouldn't that only make us more lost?"

"Not exactly," Kylie said. "As long as we pay attention to the map itself as we try out whichever route is outlined on it, we'll be able to make our way back here to retry as many times as we need. The real issue is going to be time. We really need to beat this game before nightfall."

"So let's try one right now," Matt said, goose bumps flourishing over his arms and back at the idea of being in the maze after sunset. "Let's hurry while still being careful."

"Follow me," Kylie said, raising her chin bravely, and Matt felt proud of her for facing her fear so head-on.

They tried the map with the red route first, which led them straight into a dead end. Then they tried the map with the green route, and just as it started to look as though this might be the real map and escape was imminent, the path closed off in yet another dead end.

"That means the blue map has to be the one," Miguel said as they all followed Kylie back to the clearing with the treasure box to try it. "We're going to get out of here, and soon."

Sure enough, the map with the blue route led them farther

than either of the others had, and eventually, the path finally opened up into an exit, causing everybody to cheer. But Matt noticed almost immediately that they weren't back near the house at all—the map had led them to the other side of the maze completely.

"What are we supposed to do now?" Miguel asked in exasperation. "How is this really an escape if we're still this far away from the house?"

"I'm guessing it has something to do with that," Kylie said, pointing to an old iron gate nearby that was overgrown with various flowers. Matt looked over to what she had found there, his mouth opening in surprise when he spotted it.

There, hooked over one of the sections of the flowery iron gate, was a big silver lock. Attached to the lock, there was a folded-up note, the all-too-familiar GM symbol stamped over the front.

CHAPTER 9

Becca

"What are we supposed to do now?" Frankie said, looking around in panic for alternate ways to get out of the house. "We can't just be locked in here forever!"

"Let's check the windows," Becca suggested. "And see if there are any more doors in the house that we could try besides the front door."

Danny moved from window to window, using his free hand to try to open them, and Becca did the same on the other side of the room—all were locked. Frankie made their way around the back edge, around the giant red stains on the floor, stopping in their tracks when their eyes fell upon something.

"What is it, Frankie?" Becca said from where she stood near the front window, which was just as stuck as all the others. "Do you see a door?"

"I do," Frankie said. "It's . . . already open. There's a staircase going down into pitch darkness. I'm pretty sure it's a basement."

"A *basement*?" Danny cried out. "You know there'll def be creepy crawlies in there!"

"Maybe that's where we're supposed to go next," Becca said, her skin crawling at the idea of going into a dark, spider-infested basement.

"Probably," Frankie agreed. "Maybe there will be a light we can turn on down there."

With bated breath, the friends made their way to the basement door and slowly went down the cold cement steps one by one. With every step the air got chillier and smelled wetter, an awful combination of mildew and dirt, and Becca was reminded of the time the basement at the gymnastics center flooded with slimy creek water that ruined everything it touched.

"It reeks down here," Frankie complained. "And I can't see anything."

"Hold up a minute," Danny said. "I turned on the night vision switch on my camera. I think I can see a light switch up ahead."

A few moments later, there came a clicking sound, and the

basement lit up with a dull yellow glow, not bright enough to see *well*, but it was at least enough to make most of the enormous room visible. Danny stood beneath a single dingy light bulb that hung down from a thin silver chain on the ceiling. As the light swung back and forth, the shadows of the basement moved and slithered, causing Becca to shiver.

"I can almost hear Miguel in my ear right now," Frankie said, stepping away from a moss-covered wall near the steps. *"A dark, wet environment like this would be the perfect home for a wide range of bugs. Including spiders."*

"Ewww." Danny wiped against his pants the hand he'd used to turn on the light bulb. "Everything in here is damp."

"So why did the Game Master have us come down here?" Becca wondered out loud, looking around to see if she could spy anything out of the ordinary. There, lined up on a table against one of the back walls, was a set of big jars, each with different labels that Becca couldn't quite make out from where she stood. "What are those?"

Danny hurried over to get a close-up of the jars with his camera, making sure to spend enough time on each so the audience could read all the labels in full. Becca and Frankie walked up to join him, bending down as they studied the labels.

"Eight different jars for eight different types of bugs," Danny said in a low voice. "But each jar is empty. I'm not sure I like where this is going."

"Me either," Frankie agreed. "Look, there's a note tucked beneath this first jar. Maybe it'll be the instructions from the Game Master."

Sure enough, the folded note was stamped with the familiar GM symbol. Becca opened it and read it to the others.

"Welcome, Danny and friends, to your very own creature feature! Can you identify and capture each of the basement creepies listed below? I've provided a means for a closer look, so you can get up close and personal with the stars of the show."

"Means for a closer look?" Danny wondered. "What does that mean?"

"What's this?" Frankie asked, picking up what looked like a small weight. "I think it's a microscope!"

"I am not looking at a spider through a microscope," Danny said, taking a few steps back from the table. "No way, no how!"

"It looks like only one of these jars will need to contain a spider," Becca said as she inspected the jars further. "The last jar is the spider jar, but there are a whole lot of others that come before it that don't seem so bad. See how each of the jars have 'number of legs' specified? Only one jar says eight."

"That offers very little comfort," Danny said, "when this jar over here says 'thirty to ninety pairs.' Thirty to ninety *pairs* of *legs*? What sort of monsters are we expected to deal with here?"

"I bet you that one is a millipede," Frankie remarked.

"I've seen them in my grandma's basement, and I had to help Miguel catch one for a science project once. I remember him talking about the thirty to ninety pairs of legs."

"So we're supposed to capture a millipede in that jar?" Becca asked. "Yikes."

"We can do this," Frankie said, stepping forward to grab the first jar, which listed the characteristics of a millipede. "Come on."

"You guys go ahead," Danny mumbled, bringing the camera up again to catch Frankie at the start of the hunt. "I'll just make sure everything gets documented."

"Okay," Becca said, taking a breath to steady her nervous heart. "The jar says that in addition to thirty to ninety pairs of legs, we're also looking for something that has antennae, and is 'long and wormlike.'"

"I'm not going to lie," Frankie said, kneeling in a particularly shadowy corner of the basement. "They look pretty horrifying."

When Danny pointed his camera light to the corner Frankie was kneeling in front of, there came a frantic scatter of movement over the wall, which caused Frankie to cry out and jump back. Becca fought the urge to scream at the sight of hundreds of skittering bugs, all crawling over each other to try to get away from the bright light of Danny's camera.

"So we've found the bug corner," Becca said. "See any millipedes?"

"I do." Danny's voice shook as he shifted his weight back and forth. "Right there, sticking out from underneath that piece of old cardboard."

Becca spotted the cardboard and lifted it up, grossed out at the sight of a long, tube-shaped bug with so many moving legs that she couldn't even begin to try to count them all. "I don't think we need the microscope to confirm what this one is," she said, standing back as Frankie rushed forward with the open jar.

"Got it," Frankie said, standing proudly to showcase the millipede inside the jar. It ran in confused circles around the bottom of the jar before settling to nibble at the piece of rotting wood that had been placed inside.

"Okay." Becca followed Frankie and Danny back to the table with the jars on it. "One jar down, seven to go. I think we'll be able to find all the others around that same corner. We just have to know what we're looking for."

The second jar specified that the correct bug had six legs, was oval shaped, had antennae, and was approximately one to two inches in size. The first oval-shaped bug they saw lacked antennae and was too small to fit the description, but then Becca spied a group of hungry cockroaches scurrying over an old can of dog food and knew she'd found the right answer.

Catching a cockroach turned out to be filled with much more darting around and squealing than catching a millipede, but eventually Becca got one and was able to move on to the next jar.

Before they knew it, they had filled five more jars: termite, pill bug, cricket, centipede, and earwig. The pill bug and the earwig had required the use of the microscope, which Becca and Frankie took turns with, putting the end of the scope against the bottom of the glass so they could try to count the legs.

"There's only one more jar to fill," Becca said, turning to Danny. "The spider jar."

"And?" Danny asked, zooming in on her expression.

"And I think you should do it," Becca said. "This game was clearly made for you, so you could conquer your fear. I think maybe it'd be good for you to prove to yourself that you can do it."

"Yeah," Frankie added, stepping up beside Becca. "I agree with Becca. Don't let the Game Master tell you what you are or aren't afraid of!"

"But, I mean," Danny said, unsure, "I am for sure afraid of spiders."

"Look at this description," Becca said, raising the spider jar and pointing out the characteristics on the list. "It's just a daddy longlegs spider. They're like, the most gentle type of spider there is. They couldn't even bite you if they wanted to."

Danny stood in silence, and Becca could tell he was considering it.

"You're brave, Danny!" Frankie encouraged, taking the jar from Becca to put it in Danny's free hand. "Here, I'll even film you as you do it. The audience will love this!"

To Becca's pleasant surprise, Danny didn't even try to talk his way out of the task. He took the jar and handed over the camera, his brow furrowed seriously as he approached a web-covered bookshelf.

"Come on, Danny," he said under his breath, giving himself a pep talk. "I bet the Game Master didn't expect you to agree to do this, huh?"

Becca watched Danny, inspired by his bravery. He was going to conquer his fear and catch a spider!

Using a stick from the floor, Danny carefully pulled the webs aside until he spotted a group of daddy longlegs and captured one in the jar without much difficulty. It wasn't until he came back to return the jar to Becca that she noticed the sheen of sweat on his forehead and the way his hands were shaking. As soon as the lid was on the jar, Danny took a huge sigh of relief, and Frankie and Becca burst out into a victory cheer.

"I knew you could do it!" Frankie cried out. "And that marks the last jar of the puzzle. We beat another round of the game! But now what?"

Suddenly, Becca felt something strange underneath the spider jar. Confused, she turned it over, only to spot a small, flat piece of paper taped to the bottom. "Whoa," she said, peeling it off carefully before setting the spider jar down with the others. "I think it's another clue or something!"

Danny pointed his camera over Becca's shoulder as she opened the clue to find yet another list of insect characteristics, like the ones on the other jars.

"*Weaves silk in trees,*" Becca mumbled under her breath as she read the clue. "Is that another type of spider?"

"Weird," Frankie said. "And there isn't even a jar for us to capture it in? That doesn't make sense."

"Maybe," Danny said, looking up from behind the lens, "we're supposed to go outside for it."

"Great thinking," Becca agreed. "Let's head back upstairs and see if we can get outside with the others! Maybe there will be something in that big tree out front."

Becca and Frankie rushed to go back up the stairs, and when Becca turned around to see if Danny was following them, she smiled at the sight of her friend looking proudly over the basement, his satisfied grin proof that he felt much better leaving this room than he had coming into it.

"I'm coming," he called up to her when he noticed her watching. "Let's get out of this creepy old house."

CHAPTER 10

Matt

"Another clue already?" Matt stepped forward and grabbed the note from the locked gate. "That maze was really hard to beat. The least the Game Master could have done was give us a minute to breathe before throwing us right back in to another game."

"At least it's moving along," Kylie said, pointing at the note so Matt would open it. "Let's see what waits for us next. I'm guessing that whatever it is will end with us unlocking this gate. That's the only way to get out of the maze without going back through the unmapped area."

Matt opened the note, Miguel looking curiously over his shoulder.

Well done on defeating the labyrinth, the note said. *But can you find the key to unlock the gate?*

"Told you," Kylie said with a smirk. "Already one step ahead of the Game Master."

The only other thing the note contained was a poem that Miguel read out loud from behind Matt.

> **Roses are red,**
> **Violets are blue,**
> **You need a key,**
> **What shall you do?**
> **Find the flower that holds the power**
> **to get you through the gate—**
> **and you'll be one step closer**
> **to discovering**
> **beloved Elephant's fate.**

"Elephant!" Miguel cried out. "We must be really close! Why isn't there any mention of Nacho, though?"

"Nacho must be included in a different clue," Kylie theorized. "One that comes after this. Or maybe one that the other group has already figured out."

"Yeah," Matt said, turning once again to look for any sign of the house behind the maze, just as unable to find it as he was the last time he checked. "I wonder how it's going inside the house, what sorts of things the Game Master has set up in there."

"It must be something as hard as figuring out this maze was," Kylie said. "Especially if we haven't heard any of them yelling to us from the backyard yet."

"We won't let this game almost get us like the maze did." Matt turned back to the clue, determined to get started with the game so it could end already. The sun was starting to sink lower in the sky. If night fell before they could find Elephant and Nacho, who would have the courage to stay and keep trying? Even the Game Master had hinted that staying after dark was a horrible idea.

"*Find the flower that holds the power,*" Matt read from the poem. "Does that mean that the key to the gate is hidden in one of these flowers?"

"But there are way too many flowers here," Miguel said, looking with uncertainty down the long length of the iron gate, which was completely covered and surrounded with bright flowers of all different kinds.

"It really is an impressive variety," Kylie said, looking over the spread. "Just from here I can see roses, violets, daisies, and jasmine. There even might be some poppies."

"Whoa." Miguel was impressed. "How do you know how to identify all these different types of flowers?"

"My mom is . . . a little bit of a gardener," Kylie answered with a laugh. "And by 'a little bit of a gardener,' what I really mean is 'she enters the flower show at the county fair every year and always wins the blue ribbon.'"

"Awesome," Matt said, and Miguel nodded. "Still, though, how are we supposed to check each and every flower on this gate? It's like Miguel said, there are too many. It'd take us hours!"

"Not if we organize the search a little bit," Kylie said, ignoring the flowers now to take a look at the entire length of the gate. "If each of us searches a section, we'll cover the entire gate in thirty-three percent of the time it would have taken if we'd stuck together to check."

"Thirty-three percent of the time sounds great to me," Miguel said. "Which third do you want to do?"

"I'll do the first third," Kylie said, walking down the left side of the gate and standing in a spot a third of the way down. "I'll search from the start of the gate to here. Miguel, you search from here to where Matt will begin. Matt, go stand a third of the way from the very end."

Matt shuffled over until he was standing in front of the spot where Kylie had directed him. Using sticks from the ground, each of them carved a line in the dirt to mark the places where each third began.

After that, it was a matter of patience. Everybody worked silently, using their eyes and their hands to thoroughly search each and every flower bud, some of them soft and delicate, others thick and waxy, most of them dotted with beautiful ladybugs that ate any stray aphids hungrily. Matt was mesmerized by the bright, vivid color of the flowers and the beautiful fragrance that filled his nose.

"There have been worse games to play," he called over to Kylie and Miguel, who laughed in agreement.

Even despite getting to be up close and personal with so many gorgeous flowers, the charm of the game wore off before too long. Matt's legs burned from all the kneeling and crouching, and he thought that he might be allergic to one of the types of flowers, because all of a sudden he couldn't stop sneezing. From somewhere to his left, he heard Miguel yelp as he ducked to avoid an irritated bumblebee.

"Keep going," Kylie called to them. "I know it's tedious, but we have to stick with it or we're never going to find the key."

"What would happen if we just tried to climb over this gate?" Miguel wondered, stepping back to take in the scale of the black iron gate. "Just skip the key altogether?"

"There's no way we could do that safely," Matt advised, looking at the pointy tips of the gate that reached into the sky like swords. "The key is the only way, unless you want to go back into that maze of weeds."

"No thank you," Miguel said, moving back to the spot of flowers where he'd left off. "I'd rather search the flowers."

They continued to work as quickly as they could. Matt

wondered again what Becca and the others were up to in that creepy old house. He let his imagination run wild as far as what sorts of things they might have encountered in there—ghosts, werewolves, vampires. Whatever was in there, he knew Becks would be able to handle it, and the others, too. He just hoped that whatever they were doing wasn't taking nearly as long to complete as the stuff his team had gone through so far. Maybe soon they'd all be able to get back together again.

"I think I found it!" Miguel cried out, reaching his arm deep into a thicket of roses. "Wait, sorry, never mind. It was just a snail."

Matt had to laugh as he watched Miguel put the snail back with a wince on his face, wiping the snail slime on his pants before continuing to search. Kylie looked so deep in her search that Matt panicked for a moment—what if he hadn't been doing as thorough of a job as he'd thought he was? What if the key was in his section and he already passed over it? Suddenly filled with paranoia, Matt wasn't sure if he should continue working down the line or if he should start completely over.

No. Starting over would only add more time to the game. Matt had to trust himself to have concentrated well enough not to miss the key—it's not like he *completely* blanked out when he had been thinking about Becca and the others.

Nodding to himself, he continued into a patch that was thickened with bright-red poppies. The blossoms themselves were too delicate to grab, but Matt made sure to run his hands down the stems to see if there was anything tied to them or settled into the dirt below them. When he was almost done with the section of bright red, he noticed that one of the poppies looked . . . different from the others.

Carefully, Matt poked his finger into one of the petals of the strange poppy, letting out a small sound of surprise when he realized it was made out of plastic, unlike its very real counterparts. "What the heck?" he whispered, right as he spotted a bright-red key taped to one of the petals. The key was the exact same color as the rest of the poppies, and it blended in so well, Matt knew he was lucky to have noticed it.

"I found the key!" he cried out, peeling it from where it was taped to the fake poppy petal. "It was in the poppies!"

"I always knew poppies were my fave," Kylie remarked, still out of breath from running over from her own area. "Now we can open that lock and see where the gate leads us."

"One step closer to Elephant!" Miguel said with a cheer. "Well done, Matt."

With a smile, Matt unlocked the silver padlock on the gate, and the group was able to walk through into a narrow but well-maintained walkway that went around the side of the labyrinth, back toward the direction of the house. Before they knew it, they were passing the yard itself—but they weren't in it, and could only see it from the gated walkway. His breath in his chest, Matt let his eyes move forward to see where the path would actually lead them.

There, at the end of the dirt walkway, was a side door leading directly into the house.

CHAPTER 11

Becca

"Let's go see if the front door is unlocked now that we've beaten the game in the basement," Becca suggested as she led the group into the main house again. She hustled over to the front door, only to discover it was still locked. "Darn."

"How are we supposed to go find a silkworm if we're still stuck in here?" Frankie said, looking in frustration out one of the filthy windows. "There aren't silkworms inside."

Becca looked around. "Hey, maybe we could try to go through the kitchen," she said. The group went back toward the basement door, passing it this time in order to make their way into the dingy kitchen. Right away, Becca bolted to the window over the sink to see if it was unlocked; it wasn't.

Neither was the back door beside the trash can.

Danny took his time filming all the details from the kitchen—the dirty tile floor, the antique chairs that surrounded a tiny table, the old magnets on the fridge, which Becca assumed was not running. The sink was filled with dishes that were smeared with old food. Becca thought she spotted a bit of mold in the corner of the sink and felt a little sick.

"Gross," she said, turning again to the window to see if she was able to spot the other group. Strange, she could see the short length of dirt behind the house, but no sign of Matt, Kylie, or Miguel anywhere. "I wonder what the others are doing."

"Probably something significantly less gross than this," Frankie said, looking around the room in disgust. "What sort of cook lets their kitchen get this filthy?"

"Who even knows how long all this stuff has been here," Danny pointed out, moving the camera to face Frankie. "It could be years."

"We need to find a way outside if we want to find a silkworm," Becca said, thinking as she surveyed the rest of the room.

"Whoa," Frankie said suddenly from the other side of the room. "Did anyone else notice this stuff on the counter?"

Becca turned to look—there, on the counter in front of Frankie, were a few things that seemed desperately out of place with the rest of the kitchen. There was a clean, brightly colored plastic package of some kind along with a big clay flowerpot filled with soil. "This stuff looks like it was put here recently," Frankie said as Danny filmed the spread. "Like, really recently."

"Maybe even while we were in the basement?" Becca said nervously. "Someone could be in the house watching us right now."

The group fell into an uncomfortable silence as everybody considered it. "I don't see anybody," Danny finally said. "But who knows how many places there are to hide here."

"Look," Frankie said, picking up the brightly colored plastic package. "We found our worms—and they're of the gummy variety!"

"Nice!" Becca stepped forward to look at the package. "That's kind of cool."

"It is," Frankie agreed, setting the candy down again. "I might be more inclined to try one if we weren't in this kitchen."

"Seriously," Becca said. "So then what's with the pot of dirt?" She went closer to inspect the pot, turning it around slowly. "Wait, there's a note here!" Taped to the back of the clay flowerpot was a piece of paper with the GM symbol on the outside.

Inside the note, at the top of the paper: *What is Frankie DiMarco afraid of?*

"Uh-oh," Danny said, making sure to get Frankie's reaction to the note in his shot. "Looks like it's Frankie's turn to get spooked now."

"Oh great," Frankie said, looking at the pot of soil with a different look on their face. "Just great."

"What?" Becca said, confused. "What is it, Frankie?"

"That dirt." Frankie's eyes did not move from the giant pot of black grainy soil. "It's not actually dirt."

"What do you mean?" Becca asked, still not getting it. Frankie was afraid of dirt?

"I'm most afraid of unfamiliar food," Frankie explained. They looked at the pot warily. "A chef likes to know how their food was prepared. It's just how I am. I don't like to eat something unless I know exactly how it was made."

Becca noticed that Danny was back to filming the note in her hand. Looking down, she saw that there was more written beneath *What is Frankie DiMarco afraid of?*

"*Frankie knows about all types of food,*" she read out loud. "*But what do they know about king cake?*"

"Noooo," Frankie said, covering their face with their hands. "Not a king cake."

"What's a king cake?" Becca asked, confused, then read the rest of the note: "*Frankie must eat dirt.*"

"A traditional king cake," Frankie said with a sigh, "is baked with a small item inside, usually a small plastic baby, as weird as that sounds."

"A baby cake?" Danny asked, raising his brow. "Now that *does* sound weird."

"Whoever ends up getting served the piece with the baby in it gets good luck for a year," Frankie went on. "Or, depending on which tradition you're following, has to be the one to provide the king cake at the next party."

"I'm still having a hard time connecting the dots between the cake and the clue about the silkworms," Becca admitted, looking at the package of candy on the counter. "And what does the big pot of dirt mean?"

"It's a dirt cake," Frankie said. "The note said Frankie must eat dirt. Watch this." They stepped forward, sunk their fingertips into the dark soil, and plucked out a gummy worm that'd been hidden below the surface. The gummy was covered in a thick, gooey brown—was that chocolate pudding?

"I'm pretty sure there's going to be something hidden in this dirt cake," Frankie said. "Maybe a key to get out of here or something."

Becca noticed something that she hadn't noticed before. Tucked behind the big pot was a napkin, and on top of the napkin were three spoons that were sparkling clean.

"No way," Frankie said when their eyes followed Becca's stare to the spoons. "No way I'm touching this cake. We have no idea who made it, or how they made it."

"I don't know, Frankie," Danny said, getting a close-up of the cake. "I tried a dirt cake once at a birthday party, and it was pretty delicious."

Becca had to admit that a cold chocolate treat sounded amazing right about now. "I mean, there are worse games to play," she said, taking the spoons and handing one to each person. "The only way through is through."

"Wait," Frankie cried out in panic. "No, please, there has to be another way!"

"We all agreed to do what we could in order to save Elephant and Nacho," Danny said seriously, turning the camera to Frankie. "I had to catch a spider in a jar. All you've got to do is eat a yummy dessert!"

"The Game Master wouldn't want to poison us," Becca joined in. "He enjoys toying with us too much. We just have to eat our way to find whatever is hidden in the cake. You can do it."

Frankie stared back and forth between the spoon and the cake before reluctantly taking the spoon. "Fine," they said. "For Elephant and Nacho."

"That's the spirit!" Danny said, and they all grabbed their spoons and dug in.

Becca hated to admit how delicious the first bite was. The

concoction was layered with pudding, gummy worms, and chocolate cake. There was something a little crunchy, too, maybe some sort of crushed cookie. Either way, she could get used to this game.

After about five minutes, the cake stopped being fun and became a real challenge. Becca was getting full, and she could tell from the looks on her friends' faces that they were feeling about the same way. "I'm not sure how much longer I can do this," Danny said, sounding defeated. "That is a *lot* of cake."

"Let's keep pushing it just a little farther," Becca insisted, scared about what might happen if they got too full or even got sick before they found whatever was waiting for them somewhere in the mush of chocolate and gummies. "It can't be much longer now."

Suddenly, Frankie made a weird noise, reaching into their mouth with their fingers and turning away so Becca and Danny couldn't see them. After spitting something out into their hand, Frankie ran over to the sink to try to rinse it off, but the water wasn't turned on.

"Here," Becca said, rushing forward with one of the water bottles from her backpack. They poured the water over the item in Frankie's hand, washing the remnants of chocolate cookie away until it was clean.

It was a key.

"You did it!" Danny said, zooming in on Frankie's bewildered face. "And you did it without swallowing the key."

"Seriously," Frankie said, breaking out into giggles. "Can you imagine if I had?"

Filled with the excitement of beating yet another game, the group tried the key on the back door by the trash can, but it didn't work.

"I don't get it," Becca said with a frown.

What was the key supposed to unlock?

CHAPTER 12

Matt

Matt, Miguel, and Kylie stepped up to the door leading into the side of the house, looking nervously at the note that was taped to it. The GM symbol seemed to mock them from where it was boldly stamped on the front of the paper.

"I almost wish we could just go in without reading the note," Matt said half-jokingly. "But you just know there's vital info in there."

"Exactly," Kylie said with a sigh. "I'm not super excited about the idea of going inside this house, but at least we'll be able to join up with the others again. If I ever have to look at that backyard again, it'll be too soon."

Miguel took the note from the door and unfolded it slowly.

His face drained of color as he read it, keeping silent as Kylie and Matt looked on expectantly.

"Well?" Matt said. "What does it say?"

"Just one thing," Miguel said, turning the note so his friends could see.

What is Miguel Córdova afraid of?

"Uh-oh," Kylie said. "The clue in the maze asked what I was afraid of. I guess this means that whatever comes next will revolve around whatever Miguel is most afraid of."

"It better not," Miguel sputtered, looking at the door with sincere mistrust. "If the Game Master actually wants to be our friend, this is not the way to do it!"

"What are you afraid of?" Matt asked. "Just remember that whatever it is, we're here with you. You're not going to have to do anything alone. Just like with Kylie's clue."

"My fear is super common." Miguel looked in dismay to the note. "But that doesn't make it any less terrifying for me. You see, when I was a kid, my parents took us to the shore for a beach day. Angel and I were having the best time—at first."

"Sunburn?" Matt guessed, trying to think of what could go wrong at the beach. "Sharks?"

"Water," Miguel said simply. "When we tried to go swimming, I went a little too far out. The waves started getting stronger. They started pulling me back toward the ocean, like it was trying to eat me. I started choking and sputtering on the salty water. The harder I fought to get to shore, the farther away I was pulled. If it wasn't for the lifeguard who had been watching over us, I would have drowned."

"Oh my gosh," Kylie said, her eyes wide. "I'm so sorry, Miguel. That sounds absolutely horrifying."

"Ever since then, I've been afraid of going in the water," Miguel went on. "Not just the beach. Swimming pools, lakes, even bathtubs. I just hate that feeling of being in water, that wet dog feel. It's terrible!"

Matt gulped and looked at the closed door, nervous about what might be waiting for them on the other side.

"I don't think I can go through that door," Miguel whimpered, sitting down on a bench that was alongside the gate. "I feel like if there's something we have to swim through, I might pass out."

"No," Kylie said, kneeling before Miguel. "Listen to me. If there's a swimming pool at this house, it'd be outside, not inside. I really doubt there's anything in there bigger than a bathtub. It's just like what Matt said—we're going to do it together, whatever it is. We won't let anything happen to you."

"You can do it, Miguel," Matt encouraged. "Just think about Angel's face when he sees Elephant again for the first time in months. Think about how happy you'll be to have Nacho slithering up your arm to your neck again. We're so close!"

At the mention of his little brother and the missing

animals, Miguel sat up a little straighter, looking less defeated than before. "You're right," he said. "We are close. I can feel it."

"Totally!" Kylie helped Miguel stand, and they looked back to the door. "The Game Master hasn't got anything over us. We've beaten every game thrown our way so far! I have no doubt we'll get through whatever is waiting for us on the other side of that door too."

"Okay," Miguel said with a nod. "Here goes nothing."

Matt reached forward and used the red key to open the door, which swung aside to reveal a small, darkened room filled with a long wooden bench, an old sink that was empty and stained yellow and brown on the inside, and baskets filled with dust-covered clothes. A filthy jacket hung from a hook on the wall.

"This is a mudroom," Matt said as they all stared from the outside. "It's where you take off dirty shoes and hang your coats and stuff like that."

"What does that have to do with water?" Miguel asked nervously, eyeing the empty sink on the side of the room. "That thing looks disgusting, by the way."

"It smells weird in there," Kylie noted. She crinkled her nose at the mud-streaked tiles across the threshold of the door.

"Yeah," Matt agreed. "I think I'll be keeping my shoes on, thanks."

The three laughed nervously, with everyone avoiding taking the first step inside.

"We should probably, you know, go in," Kylie said.

"Okay." Miguel bounced a little on his toes, as though hyping himself up. "Let's go!"

Matt counted down backwards from five, and they all went at the same time through the door.

As soon as they stepped over the threshold, something felt wrong. Matt was the first to notice the sound of straining rope, and the fresh water droplets that were sprinkled on the tile beneath their feet. "What was—" he started to say, looking at Miguel at the exact same moment that a huge wave of muddy water poured over all of their heads.

The cold shock of the water made Matt freeze in place, and he felt Miguel do the same at his side. The water continued to pour over them, showing no sign of stopping, and for one panicked moment Matt felt like he was going to run out of breath. He reached over and grabbed Miguel's arm, hoping that his friend wasn't freaking out even more than he was right now.

Just as suddenly as it started, the water stopped, and the three friends were left shivering and sputtering in complete shock, the overturned buckets hanging upside down over them, knocking against the door frame over and over.

Erupting into simultaneous screams, Miguel, Matt, and Kylie sprinted forward into the house. They darted through a dark hallway, Matt almost tripping over his own feet before he turned a corner and almost ran directly into someone who was standing in the living room—Becca!

"Becks," Matt gasped, dripping all over the carpet, Kylie and Miguel coming to a stop behind him in the same condition. "We found you!"

Becca stared in shock, her mouth open as she took in the sight of them all covered in water and mud. Behind her, Frankie was watching with their hands over their mouth, and Danny was filming them all with raised eyebrows.

"So I take it you've all had run-ins with the Game Master as well?" Danny finally asked, breaking the silence. "We've been through some stuff in here, but it looks like you might have been through a *teensy* bit more."

At the words of his friend, Miguel burst out laughing, wheezing as he brought his hand over his stomach while he tried to stop. This made Kylie start to giggle, then Matt. The three laughed harder and harder as Becca and the others looked on with an amused look on their faces.

"Sorry," Miguel finally managed as he started to quiet down. "Well, at least I can say that I've faced my fear now. I don't have to worry about any of the other clues trying to drown me."

"You found personalized clues, too?" Becca asked, perking up at the mention. "So did we!"

Matt shivered in the chilly darkness of the living room,

looking around at the old décor and startling stains on the carpet. "What's been going on in here?" he asked, noticing for the first time that Becca, Danny, and Frankie's clothes were all rumpled and dusty, and was that *chocolate* on the front of their shirts?

Now it was Becca's turn to laugh. "Quite a bit," she said. "Let's start at the beginning."

CHAPTER 13

Becca

"So what happened out in the backyard?" Becca asked Matt, still shocked at the sight of him and Kylie and Miguel.

Now that the adrenaline of getting cold water dumped on them was wearing off, Matt's group didn't look like they wanted to laugh anymore. Becca felt bad for them—it must be miserable to be soaking wet in your clothes! Also considering the fact that the water had been filthy, she was willing to bet that Kylie, Matt, and Miguel would have given anything for a hot shower and a clean pair of pajamas—and to be in their own homes.

"At first, it looked like there wasn't much to be seen," Matt started. He made his way slowly around the living room to check out all the stuff in it, looking in disgust at the big red stains on the floor. "Just some dirt and weeds. But then the weeds turned out to form a labyrinth. We almost got lost."

Becca looked at Kylie in surprise. She knew her friend hated the idea of getting lost more than anything. "That must have been especially scary for you."

"It's funny you should mention that," Kylie said, flipping her hair over her shoulder. "Because the first clue we found, located in the center of the maze, pointed out that very thing. The Game Master left a note asking what I'm afraid of. Then the game revolved around using a map without getting lost in the process."

"We beat it eventually," Matt confirmed with a nod. "But then we had to search through hundreds and hundreds of flowers. They were growing all over this iron gate that ran along the back side of the maze."

"Matt beat that one," Miguel said with a grin. "He found a red key taped to a fake poppy."

"What happened next?" Becca asked, fascinated. Danny made sure to move the camera between people smoothly and effortlessly to get the conversation on tape. If nothing else, at least they could say for sure that this was all going to make for a spooky, exciting documentary.

"Then came my clue." Miguel shuddered; there were still droplets of nasty brown water dripping down the bottom of his T-shirt. "Asking what I was afraid of."

"Water?" Frankie guessed, crinkling their nose at the scent of the muddy water.

"Water in the mudroom," Kylie confirmed. "It poured out of giant buckets that were set over the door leading in."

"Wait." Becca made her way past Kylie and Miguel, heading back in the direction they came from. "Did you say there was another door? And that you were able to come in through it?"

"Yeah," Kylie called back, rushing to join Becca. "How could I have forgotten already? Let's get out of here!"

Becca hurried down the hall, her excitement building as she imagined getting out of this dark, creepy house for good, with its spiders and shadows and stains. But she winced when she found the mudroom—the floor was covered in nearly an inch of dirty water, and the door at the back was now closed. That couldn't be good.

"What?" Kylie said in disbelief when she saw the door. "We definitely did not close that door."

Oh no, no, no. With a chill running down her spine, Becca walked through the water to try the door. *Please open. Please open. Please open!*

"It's locked," she said in a near-whisper, and everybody groaned behind her. "All the doors in the house are locked."

They were all trapped. Again.

"No way," Matt cried out. "We're all locked in just like we were at summer school!"

The team reluctantly made their way back to the living room, and Becca was feeling especially defeated.

"The only choice is to keep playing," Becca said. "But what are we supposed to do next? My team was trying to get outside to find a silkworm tree, and we ended up with a random key instead. One that doesn't work on any of the doors."

"You never told us what happened on your team," Matt pointed out. "Fill us in so we can all move forward on the same page."

"Right," Becca said, struggling to regain her confidence. "Well, uh, we first got in and looked around the living room. Danny ended up finding a message written on the mirror in creepy red writing."

"Speaking of red," Miguel cut in, looking at the carpet warily. "Is that blood?"

"We're going with no," Frankie explained with a shake of their head. "Let's keep going with no."

Becca continued. "The message asked what Danny was afraid of, which is spiders, but before we could figure out what we were supposed to do, the door slammed shut. And locked."

"*On its own*," Frankie emphasized. "We still can't figure out how the Game Master pulled it off."

"Then we had to go to the dark, damp basement to capture all sorts of freaky bugs," Danny cut in, turning the camera to face himself. "And I'm proud to say I'm the one who completed the spider jar."

"The . . . spider jar?" Matt asked with a shiver. "That doesn't sound fun at all."

Becca nodded. "It was pretty freaky. At the end of the game, we were given a clue, something about webs and trees, but we never quite cracked it."

"Unless you count the gummy worms," Frankie said. "But that wouldn't explain the stuff about the tree."

"Did you just say gummy worms?" Kylie asked. "*Gummies?*"

"Embedded in a big flowerpot full of dirt cake," Frankie said. "We had to eat our way to find the key."

"I'm not going to lie," Matt said, looking a little jealous. "I really would have rather gotten the cake challenge than the mud-water bucket challenge."

Frankie looked at Matt from head to toe. "Yeah, even though the cake game was made to freak me out the most, I'm not so sure I would have rather done the bucket."

Becca looked around the living room, which was getting darker as the sun set farther. "We're running out of time, and we're all out of clues," she said. "Any ideas on what we should do next?"

Before anybody could say another word, the ancient television that sat across the room from the cracked coffee table came to life, filling the room with bright-green light from the glow of its screen. The loud sound of muffled signal static nearly caused Becca to jump out of her skin. Panicked and on edge, the group cried out in surprise.

Layered over the green background was the GM symbol.

"Good afternoon," a voice boomed from the television. "Soon to be evening."

Becca gasped as she recognized the voice as the one that had come over the loudspeaker that day at summer school. She remembered how confused she'd felt when she first heard it, how she'd had no way of comprehending just how twisted things were about to get. That feeling was back now, only intensified from the atmosphere of the old house.

"The Game Master," Matt whispered.

"You've played the game well . . . so far," the distorted voice continued. "But if you really want to see Elephant and Nacho again, you're going to have to follow the books to the higher ground. I've seen what makes some of you afraid—but there's still time for the rest of you."

Becca's blood went cold. There hadn't yet been a clue for her, or Matt. He looked over at her, and they exchanged nervous glances.

"Who are you?" Frankie yelled in frustration at the screen, but then the TV turned off, leaving them in the quiet darkness of the living room once again.

Becca kept looking at the television screen, as though it might flicker back on and ask her what her fear was.

"Did you hear what the Game Master said?" she asked

weakly. "They said that we'd played the game well so far. I thought we were getting a step ahead by splitting up, but it turns out that the Game Master knew we'd do that all along." She felt like she'd failed her team somehow, led them astray by making them believe splitting up would be an unexpected way to cut corners on the game.

"You couldn't have known," Matt assured her. "It *was* smart to split up, Becks. The Game Master just knew you'd figure it out, that's all."

Becca still didn't like the idea of having no control over what was happening to them. Who was this Game Master, and what did they ultimately want?

"*Follow the books to the higher ground,*" Kylie mumbled, walking in small circles as she thought it through. "*Follow the books to the higher ground.*"

"Follow what books?" Miguel asked. "I don't see a single book in here."

"That must mean there's a room in this house with books in it," Kylie said. "Or books leading up to it. Has anyone in your group tried going upstairs yet?"

Becca shivered as she thought about the staircase she'd passed in the hallway on the way to the mudroom. "Not yet," she said. "We didn't even see the stairs at first, except for the ones that went down to the basement."

"Maybe there's a library of some sort up there," Kylie said. "Old, creepy houses like this always have libraries, I feel like."

"What do you think, Becca?" Danny asked from behind the camera. "Should we brave the upstairs?"

Becca looked up the steep staircase, knowing in her gut that there was something on the second floor that was put there specifically to terrify her with her worst fear.

"We have to," she said at last, adjusting the strap of her backpack and putting her foot on the first step. "It's the only way to find Elephant and Nacho."

CHAPTER 14

Matt

The staircase was even darker than the living room, with no windows to offer even the slightest bit of light. The steps were steep, winding, and covered in a thick, dark-green carpet that reminded Matt of moss. The air felt hotter and more stifling as they made their way up, making Matt wish he had a cold soda to guzzle. At the top of the stairs was a long hallway with a few different rooms off the sides. This house was even bigger than it looked from the outside!

"Okay," Becca said from where she stood at the front of the pack. "One of these rooms has got to contain books. We should stick together while we check."

They all moved together down the hall, peeking into

rooms as they walked by. The first room was a bathroom, with an enormous stained tub with huge, creaturelike claw feet. The mirror that hung over the sink was cracked, so when you looked in it, your face got all scrambled up, as though it'd been broken into pieces and shoved clumsily back together.

"No thank you," Matt muttered as he passed by the terrible mirror, his reflection gawking back at him like Frankenstein's monster.

The second room looked like a sewing room of some sort, with piles of old fabric that were sun-stained from so many years next to an uncovered window. There was an ancient sewing machine that reminded Matt of the one his great-grandmother used to have when he was little. Only when he looked closer did he see that the windowsill by the pile of fabric was littered with dead ants.

So far, the upstairs area was proving itself to be just as alarming as the downstairs. He imagined the Game Master sneaking from room to room, hiding in the shadows and watching over them all like some sort of ghost, and he shivered at the thought. Who would ever want to spend time in a house this creepy?

Danny was the first to pass the third room off the hallway, holding his camera up as he entered to capture everything in real time.

"Whoa!" he exclaimed before stepping gingerly inside. "I

think it's safe to say that I found the library."

The rest of the friends piled into the room quickly, Matt heading in last. He was unsettled by the creaking that seemed to come from deep within the walls of the house. But when he entered the room, he knew that Danny was right: this room had to be the one. There weren't just one or two books, but hundreds. The bookshelves almost looked endless, layered in well-spaced rows across the turret-like room that expanded out from the side of the house. At the end of the room was a big window seat that overlooked the front yard, and on the wall beside it there was a big architectural drawing with a table splayed out beneath it. The drawing was old and crinkled, pinned hastily in each corner.

"Cool," Kylie said, spinning on her toes to get a look at the entire room. "This is probably my favorite room in the house so far, if such a thing is possible."

"It really makes you wonder what this place was like before it was abandoned," Becca said, walking through the shelves, running her hands over all the leather-bound spines. "Maybe it was even really nice once, when everything wasn't all broken and run down."

Matt tried to imagine the house cleaned up, without the cobwebs or layers of dust or gigantic red stains on the floor. Maybe, just maybe, it could have been cozy once, but that ship had long sailed.

"Pleasant? Let's not forget all the bugs in the basement,"

Danny joked, moving around to get as many details as he possibly could on camera. "So . . . we've found the books. What now?"

"*Follow the books to the higher ground,*" Matt repeated from the message that had played on the TV. He tried to think what the second part of the clue could mean. "Maybe there's something on top of one of these bookshelves?" But when he checked with Becca's help, they turned up nothing except more dust bunnies.

"I'm not sure if this is relevant or not," Kylie said, from where she stood in front of the architectural drawing on the wall. "But it would appear that this drawing is actually a blueprint of a house. This house, to be precise."

Everyone went to take a closer look. Kylie was right; Matt was able to see the living room, kitchen, basement, and even the backyard, all on the old drawing. He took his finger and hovered it over the area with the library. "So that means we're in this spot right now."

"Can't get much higher ground than the second floor," Kylie said. "But I'm still not sure what exactly that's supposed to mean, or how it could help lead us to another clue."

"There has to be a clue hidden in this room," Becca said, looking back toward the bookshelves. "Maybe it's in one of the books."

Matt stepped back from the drawing, only to see that the table directly beneath it also had an old piece of parchment paper on it. The paper was so old and stained that it'd camouflaged perfectly into the table—he wouldn't have seen it at all had he not backed away.

"Look," he said, pointing to the sheet of parchment on the table. "Did anybody else notice that?"

"Ooh," Kylie said, looking down and seeing the paper for the first time. "Now this definitely looks like a clue."

"What is that written on there?" Becca asked, peering down at the parchment. "It almost looks like a message, but there are words missing."

"It looks like each missing word has a label in the blank," Kylie noted. "It either says noun, verb, or adjective. I guess those are the types of words you're supposed to use. Apparently, the game is about to go full English class."

"I know what this is!" Frankie said excitedly. "It's a mad lib!"

"A mad lib?" Matt asked, confused. "What is that?"

"It's just a passage of some sort," Frankie explained. "It could be about anything really—my sister used to find them in her magazines from time to time—and you have to fill in the blanks with your own answer to get a unique finished piece."

At the top of the mad lib there was a hand-drawn GM symbol. "This is it, then," Matt said, unsure of how to proceed. "Somehow this is the next game. But how are we supposed to know what to say? How are we supposed to make up the answers if we don't know what the Game Master wants?"

"We're going to have to gather as much context as we can," Kylie said. "From the words that are already included. Usually, the person filling out the mad lib isn't the one reading it. That's how some people get wild answers that are hilarious, but since we're all able to see the rest of the words that are included, we'll be able to at least figure out the area of the cosmos it's going for."

"Exactly," Frankie said. "We should hopefully be able to piece it together little by little, if we follow the text's lead."

"Oh, you're right," Becca noted as she read over the paper. "Look at this first line: *This is the story about the history of this* _____. Noun. Taking into account the matching blueprint, I think we can assume that the missing word is *house?*"

"Yes," Kylie said, picking up a nearby pen to scrawl the word in. "But it doesn't look like all of the lines are as easy as that one was." She frowned as she read through the next one silently. "See, this one shows the definition of some word related to a record player, but I'm not sure what it could be."

Matt peered over the parchment to see what the line was. *This is the story about the history of this* house. *A man and his wife loved it so much, and lived in it for so long, that they died in it. Even after they died, they couldn't bring themselves to leave.*

"Okay," he said under his breath as he kept reading. "This is getting spooky."

"It is," Kylie agreed. "What sort of story is this, anyway?"

Their ghosts stayed behind, the puzzle went on. *They loved to play music on their* _____ , *which was a sort of old record player that was an advancement in the phonograph.*

"How are we supposed to know what the correct term is?" Danny wondered as he filmed the group hunched over the table with the parchment on top. "Do you think that's what the Game Master meant when they said *follow the books?*"

Kylie stood straight up. "Oh my gosh," she said, turning to the camera. "You're right, Danny. We're literally surrounded by potential resources that could help us figure out what the answers might be."

"It's just like when we were summer schooled," Frankie observed. They walked over to the bookshelves and started sorting through. "When we had to figure out the clue about the dumbwaiter."

Matt went to browse a different section of bookshelves, and so did the others. At first, he worried that there were too many books to have a hope of finding the correct answer, but after ten minutes of searching, Becca let out an excited little shriek.

"I may have found something," she said, pulling a thick book out of one of the shelves. "This book has a green sticker on the spine—the Game Master's signature color. And the title is *High-Tech Gadgets of Old.* And—" She flipped open to the table of contents. "It looks like there's an entire section of things used for music!"

Everybody rushed over as Becca skimmed through the chapter. "Record player," she said when she finally found the correct entry. "It says here that earlier versions included turntables, phonographs, and . . . the Victrola!"

"Victrola," Kylie repeated. "I think I've heard about those before. My aunt used to have one that she found at an antique store, I'm pretty sure."

"This book says that the Victrola was an advancement in the phonograph," Becca went on. "Word for word, just like the clue. I bet the missing word is *Victrola!*"

They rushed over and filled in the blank. "Great job, Becca!" Matt said. "Now we just have to figure out the rest of the missing spaces."

The other words seemed to be a mixture of things either taken from a book in the library's collection, or straight from the blueprint itself. The group slowly made their way through the various terms, like *pantry* and *typewriter* and *compost bin*, while also learning about the strange and sometimes downright unsettling habits of the supposed ghosts that lived in the house. Matt tried to tell himself it wasn't too scary, but anytime the house settled or made a noise, he jumped.

"Clearly the Game Master made all of this up about the ghosts," Frankie said, almost as though they were trying to convince themselves over their friends. "But if the Victrola starts playing music all by itself, I might scream."

Me too, Matt thought, clearing his throat and hoping he

didn't look as spooked as he felt.

"We're almost finished," Kylie said, wiping her forehead with the back of her hand. "There's only one blank left."

But over all the other places in the house, the end of the mad lib read, *the ghosts especially loved to hang out in one special place. A room that was above all the others, even higher than the second floor. This room, of course, was the* _____.

It was the only line in the mad lib that was underlined in green.

"A room above all the others," Frankie read out loud. "Do you think it's talking about an attic?"

"There's an attic here?" Matt asked. "Does this house ever end?" He imagined what an attic in a house like this might look like. He was starting to feel seriously claustrophobic, like the walls of the house were made of stone, trapping them all inside forever without fresh air or sunlight.

"We should only be so lucky," Kylie said as she filled in the final word of the mad lib. "Okay, we're done. I hate to say it, but having the word *attic* underlined in green could only really mean one thing. We're supposed to find it and go inside."

Matt thought he'd probably rather do anything else.

CHAPTER 15

Becca

"Well," Becca said, "at least we know exactly where to look to find out where the attic is located."

"Exactly," Kylie agreed, looking up to study the blueprint on the wall above the table. "Let's see here . . ."

Becca's mind spun in nervous circles as she watched Kylie run her finger over the drawing, trying to find anything marked *Attic*. The mad lib clue hadn't been designed for Becca specifically, so that meant that there was something still waiting for her, somewhere in this house. She remembered the story about the two ghosts from the story on the parchment and shuddered. She could only hope that whatever was waiting for them in the attic was reserved for Matt. *Sorry, Matt,* she thought as she turned to look at him. He gave her an enthusi-astic thumbs-up, despite looking like he was feeling a little bit ill. At least she wasn't alone in her feelings.

"Found it," Kylie said after a few more moments. "It looks like the attic is actually directly above the room we're in right now. We should look around for the entrance. The blueprint labels it as a trapdoor, so I'm guessing it'll be somewhere on the ceiling."

The group spread out to scan the ceiling, the sick feeling of dread in Becca's stomach only growing heavier with every step. She tried to distract herself by thinking about what she'd do as soon as she got out of here: go home, get cleaned up, eat whatever Dad had cooked for dinner. Tell her family good night early and head up to her room, only to watch YouTube videos from the comfort of her bed until she fell asleep, safe and warm and wrapped in her softest blanket.

It sounded like heaven.

"I think I found it," Frankie called, breaking Becca away from her daydream. *The Game Master can't keep you in here forever,* she reminded herself. *Finish strong, for your friends and for Elephant and Nacho.*

"Nice job, Frankie," Danny said. He tilted his camera up to the trapdoor outlined in the ceiling, over the back corner of the room. "There seems to be a problem, though. I'm cur-rently looking at this thing zoomed in with my camera, and it looks like there's a keyhole embedded in the door. Does anyone have a key? Matt, do you still have that red one?"

"I left it in the door to the mudroom," Matt said with a frown, nervous that he'd done something wrong. "Shoot, what if I was supposed to bring it with me?"

"It's doubtful that the same key would work on both the mudroom door and this attic trapdoor," Kylie assured him. "Maybe we missed something with the mad lib. Or maybe there was a key hidden in one of those books . . ."

Becca thought hard for a minute, then suddenly realized that she knew exactly where the key was. "Frankie," she said. "Do you still have that key from the dirt cake challenge?"

"How could I have forgotten?" Frankie cried, reaching into their pocket and pulling the key out. "It's right here."

That has to be it, Becca thought hopefully. What else would that key be for?

"Yes!" Miguel cheered. "And no searching required, very nice."

"Now the real question is, how am I supposed to reach that trapdoor?" Frankie said, walking in circles beneath it. "I mean, I guess I could climb on this bookshelf. It's really high, but I think I could do it. Maybe I could just pop my head into the attic for a minute and look around to see if I can spot anything unusual. You're in gymnastics, Becca—would you be willing to spot me?"

"Of course." Becca breathed a sigh of relief. Bless Frankie for volunteering to be the one to check out the attic first. Spotting, she could do. She could practically spot in her sleep!

Frankie carefully climbed up the shelves until they finally reached the top, the old bookshelf creaking under their weight but holding strong. Becca stood below, ready to dash and catch if necessary. Frankie took the key from their pocket and reached up cautiously to try it on the trapdoor. Becca watched as the key sank into the hole, then turned easily, the loud click audible even from down on the floor.

"It worked," Frankie cried excitedly. They pulled down on the key to create a small space between the end of the trapdoor and the ceiling, then pulled it down until a small ladder slid down to reach the top of the bookshelf. "I'm gonna peek in!"

"Be careful," Danny said nervously as he filmed Frankie. "One misstep could send you flying. We don't need *three* ghosts in this house!"

"Not funny," Frankie said. "I can't think of anything worse than being in this house forever and ever. I'd rather haunt the school—and that says a lot."

"I've got you," Becca called up to assure Frankie. "What do you see in there?"

Frankie carefully climbed up the first few steps of the ladder, poking their head in for a moment before reaching a hand inside. "There's a note from the Game Master," they called down. "I'm gonna drop it down."

A moment later, a piece of paper fluttered down, landing at Becca's feet. Matt bent down to grab it so Becca could keep her eyes on Frankie. After he opened it, Becca heard Matt suck in air through his teeth.

"What is it?" she asked without looking down. "Does it ask what your fear is?"

"No," Matt answered in a quiet voice, like he was reluctant to share whatever it was that he read. "It's asking about yours."

Becca's heart skipped a beat. "Hang on to something for a second, Frankie," she called, bringing her eyes down at last to look at the unfolded note in his hand.

What is Becca Zamolo afraid of?

"No," she whispered. "*No.*"

Becca had known this time would come. Heck, she'd even had a feeling in her gut when they first started searching for the trapdoor that this clue might finally be the one to call her out. But that didn't make it any easier to consider the answer to the Game Master's question. There's no way the Game Master could have figured out her *real* worst fear, right? Except . . . they'd figured out everyone else's.

Shoot.

"Are you all right?" Matt asked gently. "You kind of look like you're about to ralph."

"I'm fine," Becca insisted, but suddenly her stomach was

churning from fear and too much dirt cake.

"Maybe you should all come up here," Frankie called down. "I'm starting to get seriously freaked out surrounded by all this darkness. It's that stupid ghost story! I think it's getting to me."

"Stay put. We're on our way," Miguel called up, taking it upon himself to be the next to climb up the bookshelf then into the attic. After Miguel, Kylie went, and as soon as Kylie had finished, Danny followed, his camera hanging from the strap that was looped around his neck.

"Do you want to go next?" Matt asked Becca when they were the only ones left. "Or should I?"

"I wouldn't mind if you did," she whispered, fearing what might be waiting for her in the attic. "I'll come last."

"Whatever your fear is," Matt said, "I hope you know you're going to get through it. We're all here for you."

Becca's heart swelled with gratitude for her amazing friends. "I know you are," she said, at least feeling a *little* bit better from his encouragement. "And I appreciate it more than you'll ever know."

Matt grinned before scurrying up the bookshelf to meet the others. His parting words left Becca with the reenergized motivation that she needed, and she decided that she was ready. Carefully, she began her climb up the bookshelf, her foot slipping on the second step. As she got higher and higher, she tried not to look down to the floor of the library.

"Hey, Becca," Danny called down as he filmed her stepping onto the ladder to the attic. "You never did tell us what it is that you're most afraid of."

Becca bit her lip before answering, her fingers wrapped tightly around the ladder rungs as she climbed. "Oh yeah, that," she finally answered, a fresh sweat breaking out over her forehead. "The answer is clowns."

"*Clowns?*" her friends called out all together, their voices laced with the beginnings of panic.

"Clowns are absolutely terrifying," Miguel agreed. "Geez, Becca, why couldn't you have been afraid of, like, puppies?"

Becca burst out into nervous laughter as she finally finished the climb to the attic. Looking around, her eyes took a few minutes to adjust. The room was large, with thick beams that stretched diagonally over the ceiling. It was even dustier than the living room—dust bunnies and cobwebs gathered in massive clumps over the floor and corners of the room. There were a few boxes scattered here and there, unmarked and in piles.

"Does it make anyone else nervous that the only thing included in the clue was the question about what Becca was afraid of?" Miguel said. "If the Game Master is hiding up here dressed in a clown suit, I'm going to freak out."

"Uh, so would I." Frankie nodded as they stood up, finally

able to see enough. "Hey, Danny, maybe you could turn on the light from your camera."

"It's like you read my mind," Danny said, flipping the switch and standing to join Frankie. "Let's check out the attic, then."

Kylie, Miguel, and Matt joined Danny and Frankie, but Becca lingered behind, anxiously scratching at her arms as she looked around the room with darting eyes. She thought that Miguel was probably joking about the Game Master hiding up here dressed like a clown, but the very thought scared Becca so much it made it hard to walk.

She thought about the first time she realized she was horrified of clowns. Her parents had taken her to the county fair, and she'd insisted that she was big enough to go through the funhouse all by herself. They tried to talk her out of it, but she'd always been headstrong, and she assured them over and over that she'd be fine.

When they finally agreed to let her go inside, she couldn't have been more excited. She went through the shake house and the bouncy bridge without issue. But then she'd found herself in the mirror maze, surrounded by endless reflections of herself, and kept accidentally walking into the trick walls. Apparently, the people running the ride were able to see Becca struggling on the security camera and sent someone in to help lead her out.

That someone had been a clown. And Becca hadn't realized that he was there to help get her out—she was convinced that he was coming to kidnap her and drag her even deeper into the funhouse. Every time the clown had rushed forward to try to get to Becca, she screamed and darted farther into the maze. Eventually, the clown chased her out of the funhouse, and she ran to her parents screaming, tears running down her face. Ever since then, she hadn't been able to even look at a clown without remembering the terror she'd experienced that night.

"There's a lot of stuff in here," Kylie noted as the bigger group moved through the attic. "It'll take us a bit to look through."

"Nacho?" Miguel called gently, as though the snake could somehow answer him. "Elephant? Are you in here?"

Becca realized that she needed to get closer to her friends. With one last look behind her to make sure there was nobody there, she stepped toward them, only to catch sight of a strange-looking box. While most of the boxes in the attic were made of cardboard, this one was made out of sturdier material, painted bright red with a yellow star on the side. "Did you see this box?" she called to her friends. "Maybe there's a clue inside."

Everybody turned back, Danny pointing the light at Becca as she approached the box curiously. At first she thought she was imagining it, but as she bent down and picked up the box to listen closer, Becca realized that there was a soft ticking noise coming from inside.

"There's something in here!" she said excitedly, right at the exact same moment that the top flew off the box loudly enough to make Becca's heart skip a beat in her chest. She realized, far too late, what a massive mistake she'd made. Immediately after the top was off the box, the top half of a terrifying clown popped up in front of her, its arms reaching, mad laughter ringing from its open mouth. Its hair was electric orange and wild, spiky, and fuzzy at the same time, and its eye makeup made it look like it was crying thick, black, inky tears. Its mouth was painted candy-apple red, the corners reaching up its face at unnatural angles. *MWAHA-HAHA!* the clown screamed over and over, never stopping, rocking back and forth as it reached for Becca.

"Becca!" Matt yelled, but she was unable to hear him over the sound of her own bloodcurdling screams.

CHAPTER 16

Matt

"Becca," Matt called again, rushing forward to help pull his friend away from the nightmarish clown. It kept rocking back and forth with its arms out, its shrill and manic laughter filling every extra inch of space in the attic. "Come on, Becks, step back, it's not real!"

"Not real?" she shrieked, looking at him in shock. There was no way around it—she was terrified. He felt awful for her.

"It looks like a giant jack-in-the-box," he said loudly, doing his best to project over the sound of the laughter, looking around the side of the box that the clown had sprouted from. "Dang, that was really something, wasn't it? Are you okay?"

Becca stared at the clown as if in disbelief, the color completely drained from her face. She was still breathing hard, her hand over her heart. "I think that is officially the most scared I have ever been in my life," she managed. "Except for the last time a clown scared me this badly, of course. But now that it's over, I feel . . . kind of good, weirdly."

"Right?" Kylie said from across the room. "Makes you feel strong, doesn't it? Facing my fear wasn't how I thought it'd be at all."

"Same," Danny agreed. "I felt pretty proud of myself after leaving that basement. I think we're all pretty cool for getting through our clues without dying of fright."

"Seriously," Frankie added, and Miguel nodded.

Matt gulped at the conversation. The group still hadn't come across any clues that were made just for him yet, but maybe the Game Master had forgotten about him. That would be the best case. He wanted to hold on to that hope, because the other option was that his worst fear was waiting for him, and he knew without a doubt that he'd rather deal with literally anything besides that. The fact that they were in an attic was already making him nervous—it had seemed like the perfect fit for his worst fear. When he'd unfolded the note that Frankie had dropped from the trapdoor, he'd been sure the clue would be for him. When it had been for Becca instead, he hadn't been able to help feeling relieved. Now that they were up here, though, he was getting uneasy again.

After the clown ran out of juice and stopped swinging around, the crazed laughter dying down until it was completely silent, Becca was able to gather herself enough to join the others in searching around the room.

"I don't see Elephant or Nacho in here anywhere," Miguel said in frustration. "We've done so much, how have we not beaten the game yet? This is getting ridiculous."

"I think we passed the point of no return in ridiculousness hours ago," Matt said with an empty chuckle. "Don't worry, Miguel, we *will* find them. There can't be too much more— we've been through the whole house now!"

"That is true," Miguel agreed, looking around the room warily. "We must have missed something in here."

"Let's keep looking," Becca said. "Maybe we should consider opening some of these boxes."

The group spread out. Matt went over to the nearest box and opened the top, afraid of what might be inside, but luckily there were no clowns or spiders to be found in the box. Instead, there were stacks of old photographs, many of them black and white. Distracted, Matt looked through a few— most of them showing a sweet old couple in various rooms in the house, smiling and laughing. In the photographs, the house looked significantly less creepy than it did now, tidy and cozy, the windows letting in much more sunlight than they currently did, caked over with filth.

Matt remembered the ghost story from the mad libs puzzle,

and goose bumps rose over his arms, making the hairs stand on end. If the story had been made up, then why were there photos of people that were like what the story described?

There's no such thing as ghosts, he had to remind himself.

Meanwhile, Danny went from person to person, filming their searching efforts before moving on, finally landing at the quieted jack-in-the-box. "Where did the Game Master even get this thing?" he asked, making sure to sweep the lens to cover every inch of the deranged clown. With the light on his camera still on, he bent over the edge of the box to try to get a shot of the inside. "Hey, there's something in here!"

They all rushed over. Matt watched as Becca took a deep breath before plunging her arm into the darkness of the box. When she pulled it back out, there was a green envelope in her hand.

"Got it!" Becca turned the envelope over.

On the front of the it, everyone's names were written right in a row—*Becca, Matt, Kylie, Miguel, Danny, Frankie*. Matt couldn't help but breathe a sigh of relief that it wasn't only his name on the envelope.

"Well done, Danny!" he said. "Who knows how long we would have searched if you hadn't thought to look inside the clown box."

"For real," Becca said, turning the envelope over to open it. "And let's all agree to never repeat the words *clown box* ever again, shall we?"

Matt had to laugh at that. He made a mental note to never let Becca forget about the clown box.

Becca removed two index cards from the envelope. Matt could see from where he was standing that each card had a question scrawled over it, in the same handwriting that had been used to write their names.

"What do they say?" Kylie asked, and Becca turned them so everybody could see.

The first card read, *What is the biggest ant in the world?*

The second card read, *What has bark but no bite?*

Matt released a breath that he hadn't even realized he was holding. Another clue given without inquiring about his worst fear. He started to feel a little less nervous than he had before.

"These are riddles," Kylie said. "Does anyone know the answers off the top of their head?"

"No," Matt confessed immediately. "Not even a little bit. I've always been horrible at riddles."

"Is that first one really a riddle, though?" Miguel asked, staring at the first card. "I mean, it looks more like a trivia question to me. The largest ant in the world is a *Dinoponera*."

"It's definitely meant to be a set of riddles," Kylie said. "Which would mean that the answer isn't going to be what it seems."

"Hmm," Miguel said. "I think you're right. I'm not sure what we would do with 'Dinoponera' anyway."

"Exactly," Kylie answered. "It has to be a play on words somehow."

The others started throwing around suggestions, but suddenly Matt became overwhelmed by the task. He was so tired from the day, and the idea of trying to squeeze any effort from his brain to try to solve the riddles seemed impossible. Letting the others get into it, he quietly stepped back, walking slowly around the attic again to try to burn off the antsy feeling of wanting to be done with the game.

"I'm just thinking on my own," he told Becca after he noticed her watching him walk around. "I swear."

"Sure," she said, the side of her mouth turning up just the slightest bit, but still she directed her attention back to the rest of the group, apparently understanding that he needed a break.

Thanks, Becks.

Sometimes he still couldn't believe that Becca had become his best friend. He had to admit that at least something good had come from the Game Master's shenanigans.

"Ant . . . think of words that have 'ant' in them," Kylie speculated. "Throw out anything you can think of."

"Chant," Danny said.

"Pants," Frankie suggested.

"Elegant," Miguel threw out. "Although 'chant' and 'elegant' don't mean anything that could be deciphered as 'big,' and 'pants' doesn't seem right, either." He thought for another second, and then his jaw dropped. "Holy cats, I think I have it—I think I solved the riddle!"

Matt approached a small window in the corner of the attic as the others buzzed with excitement. Set up in front of the window was an antique telescope, pointed in what appeared to be a very deliberate direction. He noticed that the window in front of it had been wiped clean—cleaner than any other window in the entire house had been. Was it a coincidence, or had the Game Master done it recently?

"What is it?" Becca asked. "*What is the biggest ant in the world?*"

"An *elephant!*" Miguel cried out victoriously. "The riddle is a nod to Elephant's name! Maybe we're really about to find him and Nacho, for real this time!"

"We still have to figure out the second part of the riddle," Kylie said, as Matt stepped behind the telescope and peered into the eyepiece, careful not to move it at all. "Maybe it'll tell us where Elephant and Nacho actually are."

"Good thinking," Becca said. "Okay. *What has bark but no bite?*"

Danny turned the camera toward Matt suddenly as he noticed that Matt hadn't moved from in front of the tele-scope. "What's going on over there, Matt?" he called over. "You look like you found something interesting."

"Tree," Matt responded, a wide grin slowly spreading over

his face as he took in what he could see through the tele-scope. "Tree!"

"Yeah," Becca said in a weird voice. "There are things out-side called *trees*, Matt . . ."

"No," Matt said, looking up from the telescope with a laugh. "*What has bark but no bite?* A tree. And this telescope was pointed directly at the one in the front yard. And, even better, there's a green GM symbol spray painted on one of the higher branches."

CHAPTER 17

Becca

Becca rushed over to the telescope, stepping in front of Matt to get a look. "Yes!" she cried out. "He's right. So the answers to the riddles are Elephant and tree. I can only guess that means that Elephant is in the tree."

"Didn't you mention something about a clue that never ended up landing before?" Miguel asked. "Something about silkworms and webs in a tree? Do you think that could help with this?"

"Definitely possible," Becca agreed. She frowned—they'd cracked the code of where to find Elephant, sure, but they were still faced with the same problem as before. They needed to get outside somehow, but as always, they were stuck inside.

How were they supposed to get out? She stared at the tree, thinking.

"So close, yet so far," Danny said with a sigh. "I hope we figure this out soon. I'm almost on my last battery for my camera."

"It's getting late, too," Frankie added. "I don't have much longer before I need to be home for dinner or my mom's gonna flip."

Becca nodded. There would be trouble if she was late, too—she always came home on time, so if she didn't, her parents would know right away that something was up. They'd probably get extra worried and call Matt's parents, and then Matt's parents would say that Matt hadn't gotten home yet either, and then they'd be even *more* worried.

"Same," Miguel said. "I bet Angel is wondering where the heck I am. I promised him earlier that we'd play video games today—whoops. Hopefully bringing Elephant home will be enough to make up for it, though."

"This is the last obstacle," Becca said. "That tree is the final destination, I just know it. We just have to figure out how to *get* there."

She looked out the window, picturing an imaginary trail leading from the tree to where they were now. She noticed for the first time that there was a little section of roof that protruded out from beneath the attic window. And, farther down that same section of roof, the spray-painted tree in question's tallest branches reached over to touch down on it.

"We could climb on to the tree from the roof," she whispered, looking at the attic window. Without saying another word, she reached her hand forward to push on the window—it opened! The only unlocked window in the entire house!

"You found a way out!" Miguel nearly yelled. "Yes!"

"It's not like we can just climb out the window," Matt blurted, his face suddenly a little redder in the cheeks. "That's not safe at all."

"No less safe than crawling our way into this attic in the first place," Becca said, pushing the window farther out until there was enough space for each kid to easily climb through. "All we really have to do is walk on the roof over to the tree branches, then climb over and onto it. We're all tree climbing masters already. Think of the time we wanted to paint the outside of the clubhouse! That was way more intense than this will be."

Once the window was open all the way, Becca was able to spot a note tucked into the frame. More word from the Game Master! She grabbed the note and unfolded it, reading it out loud to everybody else.

What is Matt Darey afraid of?

"No." Matt groaned, covering his still-red face with his

hands. "I'd somehow convinced myself that I'd be able to avoid having to face my fear. But of course, I was wrong. The Game Master just saved me for last, I guess."

"What's your fear?" Miguel asked, but based on how Matt had sounded at the suggestion of climbing out the window, Becca thought she probably already knew the answer to that. *Uh-oh,* she thought. *This isn't going to be easy for him—at all.*

"Heights," Matt said, hanging his head down. Becca had guessed right. She looked out the open window again and had to admit that the attic over the second floor was really high up. How would they be able to convince Matt to come with them?

A breeze came through the open window, gently blowing her hair out of her face. She inhaled the fresh air, desperate to get out of the stuffy house and leave it behind, cursed clown box and all.

"What if you just make sure not to look down?" Frankie suggested.

"We can even surround you if you want," Kylie offered. "So you don't even have to see the edge of the roof. It'll be just like walking on the ground, until we get to the tree."

"And what happens when we get to the tree?" Matt challenged. "We all just climb on to the branches and hope that nobody falls down and breaks their neck?"

"You won't fall," Becca assured him. "I won't let you. You

can climb on to the branches when there's someone both ahead of and behind you, so there'll always be somebody to hold on to, no matter which way you look. Plus, check out the roof itself—it totally slopes downward on the way to the tree. By the time we get to that back corner, we won't be three stories up anymore. If anything, it'll be more like one and a half."

Matt looked at the window, thinking it over.

"Come on, Matt," Miguel urged. "We've beaten all the games. We've pretty much defeated the Game Master, this is just the last step. Elephant has been gone for so long! Climbing down that tree will end something that was started *months* ago."

Matt looked hopefully to Becca, who offered an encouraging smile. "What do you say?" she asked him. "Do you trust us to help you get out of here in one piece?"

Matt sighed, looking out the window. "I guess I don't really have a choice," he said at last. "Because there is absolutely no way that I'm going to stay in this house a minute longer."

"Yes!" Becca clapped her hands together, proud of her best friend. They were really going to escape the terrible old house! "I'll go first," she offered. "Then everyone else can come and form a wall so that when it's your turn, you don't have to see off the edge of the roof, just like Kylie said."

"Okay," Matt said, still looking like he wanted to faint. "Let's go before I change my mind."

Desperate for escape, Becca reached her hands out the open window, holding on to the frame as she pulled herself up and over it. Suddenly she was standing outside on the roof. Turning away from the house, she marveled at the view from up here—she'd never thought she'd be so happy to be in this yard again, or, at least, in view of it. She thought of how hard she'd tried to avoid having the group come here at all and could almost laugh at herself. Look how far they'd come in just one day.

"Incoming," Kylie's voice piped up from behind her, and before she knew it, everyone was standing next to her on the roof.

Except for Matt.

"We're ready for you," Becca said gently from the lineup. "Come on out!"

Matt only trembled a tiny bit as he climbed out the window, never turning to face away from the wall, even though everyone was standing there to block the view of the drop. He shuffled to the side, motioning for everybody to follow along. The group made their way down the slope of the roof, taking care to match Matt's pace without hurrying him along, and soon they had reached the end of the line.

"All right," Becca said, looking at the branches within easy reach of the roof. "The good news is that this is going to be even simpler than we thought. There are enough branches that we'll be able to step over while still holding on to something with our hands."

"Nice," Miguel said. "You wanna go first again, Becca?"

"Sure," she answered, taking care to look as relaxed as possible for Matt's sake. They were so close, they only had to make it a little bit farther. "Here I go."

Becca stepped effortlessly over to the first set of branches, which were thick and sturdy enough to easily hold her weight. "This is great," she called back to Matt. "I could jump up and down on these if I wanted to—they definitely won't break."

"Don't jump on them!" Matt replied, his voice a little higher than usual. "I mean, I believe you, but let's not push it."

"Sorry," she said, realizing too late that jumping up and down on the branches probably did anything *but* make Matt feel more comfortable. "Anyway, I'm going to move in farther. Someone else feel free to follow me!"

Kylie came next, and after that, Miguel, Danny, and Frankie helped talk Matt through taking his turn. Once he saw the full situation with the branches, he visibly relaxed, and Becca beamed at him proudly. "You did it," she said, meeting up with him as he climbed closer to the trunk. "Now we just have to make our way slowly down."

"I'm not even sure we have to do that," Matt said, his eyes

shining as he looked at something over Becca's shoulder. "It looks like we'll be able to use the ladder coming out of that treehouse."

Treehouse? Becca whipped around in surprise, her eyes growing wider as she spotted a cube-shaped treehouse nestled deep in the branches. It blended into the tree so well it was like camouflage!

"There's a treehouse here!" Becca called to the back of the group, and everyone murmured excitedly as they all edged their way closer and closer. With all the leaves on the branches, it was no wonder that nobody had noticed the treehouse until now.

Soon enough, everyone in the group was standing safely on the deck of the newly discovered treehouse, the green GM symbol that they'd spotted with the telescope before hovering just over their heads.

"Something tells me that there'll be someone special waiting inside for us," Becca said, taking Miguel by the arm and gently leading him to the door. They'd all been waiting for this moment ever since they first discovered that Elephant had been hamster-napped after the summer school incident. "More precisely, two special someones. Would you like to do the honors of being the first to see them, Miguel?"

His head held high, Miguel reached forward and opened the door to the treehouse, stepping inside.

CHAPTER 18

Matt

"Nacho!" Miguel yelled as soon as he was inside the spacious treehouse. "Elephant! We found you! We finally found you!"

His heart still pumping from climbing from the roof to the treehouse, Matt hurried inside, excited for the safety of a stable structure. It smelled like freshly cut wood, as though the clubhouse had been built very recently. He looked to where Miguel was crouched—sure enough, sitting in the corner of the room was an elaborate hamster cage, with Elephant waiting happily inside. Nacho was in another cage that sat beside Elephant's.

Matt walked over and bent down to get a closer look; both animals looked well fed, clean, and taken care of. Elephant was even wearing a tiny black suit complete with coattails, greeting Miguel in style. "It's like hamster couture," he said.

"I missed you so much," Miguel gushed as he eagerly opened the snake cage and stuck his arm inside. Nacho instantly swirled up and around Miguel's arm, like he was giving his long-lost owner a hug.

"Awww," Becca said from where she stood watching behind them. "I'm so glad they're okay. They look happy and healthy, but still especially excited to see you."

"Angel is going to lose his mind when he sees Elephant," Miguel said, standing to interact more with Nacho as Danny made sure to get the hamster wearing a suit on camera. "I can't wait to see his face when I first get home!"

"Another game won," Danny announced in his narrator voice as he taped. "Just like with summer school, the crew managed to make their way through all the Game Master's obstacles. The tricks were aplenty, the frights were galore! All to come to a happy conclusion, closing the chapter that was oh so mysteriously opened over two months ago . . ."

"Wow," Frankie said, reflecting. "We really just did that. We went into the house on Gurley Street. It's truly hard to believe."

"Totally nuts," Becca agreed. "*And* we figured out how to escape before nightfall, thank goodness. Take that, Game Master!"

"Seriously," Matt said, looking down at the hamster, who was running around in happy, adorable circles. The inside of the cage was nice and tidy, with a bowl of fresh food and a bottle full of water available to Elephant. "I don't even want to imagine what it would have been like to do the whole roof-to-tree thing at night."

Kylie shuddered. "Now that we're out of that house, to imagine going back inside, even if just for one second, makes my insides twist around themselves!"

"Same," Frankie agreed. "Never, ever again."

Matt couldn't agree more.

"Whoa, check out this snack spread!" Danny said from behind them, and when Matt turned he was greeted by the sight of a table that held a variety of delicious-looking snacks: gummy worms, little individual cups of dirt cake, and paper cups filled with orange juice. Their victory snacks from the Game Master, no doubt.

"Yum!" Without thinking, Matt rushed forward and grabbed a cup of dirt cake, taking a big chocolatey bite that was so good it made him close his eyes. He hadn't realized just how hungry he'd become; his stomach had been too busy fighting the discomfort of being locked inside the house to notice before. Grateful, he took a big swig of juice, before turning back to the group and offering another dirt cake cup to Frankie.

"I . . . think I've had enough dirt cake for today, thanks," Frankie said with a laugh, walking over to the table beside Matt. "I'll totally take some gummy worms, though."

"I want cake!" Kylie cried as she rushed over, digging in just like Matt had. "Mmm, this is delicious!"

"I will also be choosing worms over cake," Becca said, going for the orange juice first.

The group ate their snacks for a few moments of silence. Matt was relieved that his clothes had mostly dried from the mud-water incident. Regardless, he couldn't wait to get home.

"No way," Miguel said, suddenly moving over to one of the windows carved out of the side of the treehouse. "Becca and Danny and Frankie—didn't you say one of your clues had something to do with webs in trees?"

"Yeah," Danny said. "Why?"

"Because there are wood worms living in this tree," Miguel said, amused as he pointed out a patch of webbing spread over the bark. "Just like the clue said."

"Wow," Frankie said. "It all made sense in the end, then."

Matt couldn't help but be impressed at the complexity of it all. "Dang," he said. "The Game Master really went all out for this game, didn't they? I wonder how long it'd take to plan something like that?"

It would take a long time, he realized. Maybe even up to

two months or more—just about the same amount of time that had passed since the first round of games.

"Seriously," Becca said. "That was way more intense than summer school. I'm so glad whoever it is decided to give Elephant and Nacho back for real and didn't drag it on any longer."

Matt tried to imagine how he would have felt if instead of finding Elephant and Nacho in the treehouse, they'd found another clue from the Game Master. Thank goodness that hadn't been the case!

"It just begs the question," Kylie started, pausing for a moment at Danny's request so he could fire the camera back up and get the conversation on tape. "Who would go through so much effort to set up a game like that?"

"I'm starting to feel less and less sure that it could be someone like Mr. Verdi or Vice Principal Pinter," Matt admitted, thinking it through for the first time since they'd last talked about it. "Which is to say, I have no idea who to even consider anymore. The whole thing is just way too . . ."

"Weird?" Kylie suggested. "Detailed? Yeah, I'm starting to doubt my previous guess of Mrs. Richards, too. I just can't picture her taking this much time or effort on a random group of friends. There just isn't enough motivation there for the theory to hold any water."

Matt had to agree. He felt like despite having more

exposure to the Game Master through the length of the game, he only knew less about the elusive figure. There were too many unanswered questions to even begin to untangle the web of possibilities. As he continued eating his dirt cake, he realized that it was a really good thing that he'd left Ralphie at home; the mud-water incident probably would have fried his circuitry and messed him up even worse.

He couldn't help but feel a lot of resentment over whatever the Game Master did to Ralphie. Matt promised himself again that he'd figure it out somehow, help repair Ralphie back to his fully functioning state. Watching Miguel with Nacho reminded Matt of just how much he missed his robotic friend.

"This hamster cage is really something else," Miguel said, looking over it. "It's way nicer than Elephant's old cage, to be honest, even if it's a little smaller. Between that and all the little costumes, the Game Master really pulled no punches when they went through with this." Nacho was draped around his neck, and Matt at least felt happy that his friend had been reunited with his serpent bestie. He remembered how upset Miguel had been when he first arrived at the clubhouse earlier, after discovering that Nacho was missing. Had that really only been earlier today? It all felt like it'd taken place so long ago.

"I had the same thought," Becca said. "It all just supports

the theory that whoever the Game Master is secretly wants to be our friend."

Matt didn't know how to feel about that idea. He stepped away, leaving the group to talk about the Game Master, and went to look out the window where Miguel had spotted the web worms, unable to stop thinking about Ralphie. It wasn't until he leaned against the edge of the window that he spotted something crammed into the small space between the wall and the window frame—a notebook of some kind.

"I found something," he said, reaching his fingers into the space to try to grab the sides of the notebook and wedge it upward. When he got the top of it sticking up through the space enough, Becca was able to grab the notebook and pull it out the rest of the way. It was one of those black-and-white-marbled composition books, the kind they'd been required to bring every new school year since second grade. *Notes*, it said in shaky handwriting on the front. Matt's jaw dropped at the sight of it.

"No way," Danny said. "Do you think it belongs to the Game Master?"

Hardly able to contain himself, Matt took the notebook from Becca and opened it, and all the kids peered eagerly inside.

The pages were covered in what was unmistakably a kid's handwriting. The scribbles were sloppy but impressively organized. Matt looked at the first page, which contained what looked like a mini profile of Becca. "Whoa," he said under his breath.

Becca, the top of the page read, followed by a list of accompanying facts. *Loves gymnastics. Loves her friends. Loves her nana's zoetrope.*

"Freaky," Becca whispered, and Matt turned the page to see what would come next. Another mini profile, then another, then another. There was a page for everybody in the group.

The notebook covered Matt's love of jokes and robotics, and Danny's love of filmmaking and creating. It talked about Frankie's passion for cooking, and Miguel's knack with animals, and Kylie's impressive skills with digital devices and puzzle solving. Each page had clumsily drawn but accurate cartoon versions of each of them to accompany their profiles, and another page showed a surprisingly accurate diagram of the treehouse in Becca's house. *The Clubhouse*, the page was labeled.

"How does the Game Master know what my treehouse looks like?" Becca asked uneasily. "Does that mean they've seen the inside of it before?"

Matt imagined the Game Master sneaking into the clubhouse while they weren't there, looking through all their stuff.

"And how do they know that we use Becca's treehouse specifically as our clubhouse?" Kylie wondered. "That's some serious spy work going on right there. Maybe we should set up a security camera or something."

Matt turned the pages back until he could see his own profile again. He studied the drawing of Ralphie and the notes attached, hoping to find any sort of clue that might reveal what was done to him during the summer school game.

Solid design, the notes by Ralphie read. *Motion controller. High capacity battery. Censor board. Wireless LAN AV transmitter.*

For the first time, Matt wondered if it was possible that nothing had physically been done to Ralphie, but rather uploaded through the wireless transmitter. It would explain why he couldn't find anything different whenever he went through the trouble of disassembling Ralphie to try to figure out what had happened to him.

"Should we take this notebook with us as evidence?" Kylie asked. "Or do you think it'd make the Game Master more likely to strike back whenever they discovered it was missing?"

"It's hard to say," Frankie said. "But I could easily imagine the Game Master being unhappy after discovering that it was gone."

"I've got all the pages on film," Danny reminded them.

"We can look back whenever we want. Let's put it back, just in case taking it would push the Game Master to mess with us again."

"No more games," Becca groaned. "I am so tired that my bones hurt. I'm going to sleep like a rock tonight, I can tell already."

"I need a shower," Kylie said, looking down at her soiled clothes. "My mom is not going to be happy about the mud on my shoes."

Matt looked down at his own shoes, relieved that he'd put on an older pair of sneakers this morning instead of the ones his mom had bought him just last month.

"Ugh, same." Miguel bent down to pick up the hamster cage, leaving the one Nacho had been in behind. "It's going to be dinnertime soon. Let's get out of here, team."

"Yes!" everyone said together, making their way toward the exit.

Matt waited for Becca as she went to return the notebook to the hiding place where they originally found it, but his smile turned to a frown when he realized that she'd frozen in place in front of the window, as if she'd caught sight of something horrifying.

CHAPTER 19

Becca

"Becca?" Matt said from where he stood near the exit. "What is it?" The others stopped what they were doing to look and see why he sounded so serious, the rope ladder still rolled up in Frankie's hands, ready to be dropped down the open exit on the floor.

Becca didn't move from her spot, her eyes unblinking at the sight of something mounted to one of the tree branches right outside the corner of the window, something that they'd all missed before.

"I found another telescope," she said, her voice catching in her throat. "And I think it's pointed in the direction of our houses. At the very least, it's definitely facing our neighborhood."

"What?" Miguel carefully set the hamster cage down to come see what she meant, the others following him.

Becca leaned out the window of the treehouse to look through the telescope, scared at what she might see. Her mouth dropped open when she realized that she was looking into the window of her own treehouse. "Oh my gosh," she said under her breath. "It's the clubhouse. I'm guessing this is how the Game Master knew how to draw it."

At least that meant that maybe the Game Master hadn't actually snuck into the clubhouse at some point. The idea of the Game Master in her own yard was scary. Becca backed away from the telescope, careful not to move it from the direction it was pointing so that Kylie could take a look for herself.

"No way," Kylie said as she peered through. "That is seriously freaky. It's like the Game Master has thought of everything."

Becca looked at Matt in shock. All this time, when they'd been meeting up to discuss the Game Master or whatever else, they were being watched from all the way over here, deep in the forest behind Gurley Street.

"Okay," Frankie said, a little pale. They looked at the telescope with distaste. "I don't care how good these gummies are, we need to get out of here, and now. I'm officially creeped out all over again."

Becca took one last long look through the telescope pointed to her backyard as everybody else made their way down the rope ladder, Miguel having to go especially slow with the hamster cage gripped firmly under one arm. Becca imagined that she was seeing the clubhouse through the eyes of the Game Master, watching the group's every move, plotting and planning and gathering details to use against them. She made a note to cover the big window that the telescope could so easily see through as soon as she got home.

After making sure the notebook was wedged properly back into its hiding place, she made her way down the rope ladder, going as quickly as she could manage without slipping off. The group waited for her at the bottom, with Matt on his scooter that he had retrieved from its spot near the mailbox. When she finally hopped down to the ground, she turned toward the old creepy house for one last look before she left and never came back.

The open window of the attic seemed to mock her, a stark reminder of what they'd all been through. She thought of the stale air inside the house, the giant red stains on the floor, the horrifying corner in the basement that was crawling and squirming with an endless amount of bugs and spiders. She wondered how long it would take for all the water on the floor of the mudroom to evaporate, and if the red writing on the mirror would eventually melt away.

Most of all, she wondered if the mad lib story about the ghosts living inside had been true.

Suddenly, something moved across the porch, catching her eye. Becca gasped and pointed, causing the team to turn and look. There, standing in the front window of the house, was a dark figure that cast a shadow over the porch. It moved again—there was someone standing in the house watching them!

"It's the Game Master!" Kylie shrieked at the same exact time that Frankie bellowed, "*Ghooooost!*"

Becca screamed and bolted from the house, the others following suit, Matt in the front with his scooter, Miguel trailing in the back as he held tightly to Elephant's cage. The friends ran and ran, all the way through the forest, not stopping even after the house was out of sight, only slowing when they broke out of the tree line and on to the main street.

"Who was that?" Danny cried, walking backwards to film the forest as they moved away, just in case there was anyone following them. "*What* was that?"

"I don't know, but I am never going back to that house as long as I live," Frankie said, panting as they struggled to catch their breath.

"Come on," Matt joked, also out of breath on his scooter.

"Not even on Halloween?"

"Sure," Becca said. "Right after you."

"I think I'm good," Matt said, and everyone burst into relieved laughter.

"Did anyone think they'd be facing their worst fears by force when they woke up today?" Kylie asked as they made their way down the street toward their own neighborhood. "Because I sure didn't."

"Definitely not," Miguel said. "This whole day feels like some sort of dream. Nacho disappearing, going to the house to investigate, all of it."

"A dream?" Frankie scoffed. "More like a nightmare!"

Becca smiled and took a deep breath of the fresh air, turning her face up to the late afternoon sun, basking in its warmth. "We killed it today, plain and simple. Seriously, everybody should be proud."

"We had a great leader," Matt said, swerving the scooter in big half circles back and forth across the street. "Well done, Captain Becks."

"Thank you," Becca said. "I'm just so excited to see Angel's face when Miguel walks in with Elephant."

"Same," Miguel said, stroking the spot beneath Nacho's chin as the snake nestled itself happily under the collar of his shirt. "Our family will be complete once again, for the first time since summer."

As the group approached the neighborhood, Becca remembered all of the flyers they'd posted for Elephant and Nacho before going to the house. Everybody spread out to take down as many as they could, Matt getting the most with help from his scooter, and Danny remarked that he'd never been so happy to have a flyer go out of business so quickly.

After all the flyers had been collected and stuffed into her backpack, the group finally entered their own neighborhood. Becca felt like she was looking at it with new eyes—all the houses looked so nice and tidy and normal, no shadows crawling over the walls, no mysterious figures in the windows. "Home sweet home," she yelled, raising her arms at her sides as though hugging the general atmosphere of the neighborhood.

At last, the group's cul-de-sac came into view, and everybody started walking a little faster at the promise of almost being home.

"First things first," Becca said, leading them all toward Miguel's house. "Let's go reunite Elephant with his owner."

CHAPTER 20

Matt

Matt left his scooter at the end of his own driveway before hustling over to join the others as they all approached Miguel's front door.

"Angelito!" Miguel bellowed after he stepped inside. "We have something for you, little bro!"

"What is it?" a little voice called from the living room. "I'm watching television. I'm mad at you—you promised we'd play video games this afternoon!"

"There's somebody here who wants to see you," Matt answered, and they all made their way into the living room.

Angel was laying on his belly on the carpet, his chin

resting in his hands, propped up on his elbows. When he looked over and saw that Miguel was holding an unfamiliar cage, he frowned.

"A new hamster?" he said, sitting up. "Miguel, I told you I don't want to replace Elephant, he was too special—"

"Look closer, Angelito," Miguel said. "Does this hamster look familiar, even though he's wearing a suit?"

The mention of the suit piqued Angel's curiosity. He wriggled his way up from the carpet and came over to the cage, looking inside curiously.

"Elephant!" he screamed, reaching in to grab the hamster and hold him close, kissing the top of his fuzzy little head over and over. "Oh, I missed you so much, such a good boy you are, where did you get this suit? You look like you're going to a movie premiere!"

That made Matt laugh, and the others too.

"Does this mean you beat the Game Master?" Angel said. "The one who kidnapped Elephant in the first place?"

"We sure did," Becca said proudly. "We beat the Game Master to win Elephant back. Nacho too."

Miguel smiled as Angel wrapped his arms around his brother's waist. "Thank you so much, Miguel," Angel said. "I know you always promised me that you'd find Elephant again, but you did it, you actually did it!"

Miguel squeezed the boy back. "Anything for my little

brother," he said. "It was a piece of cake, really."

"Yeah," Frankie said bitterly. "A piece of *dirt* cake."

Angel looked in confusion at the friends as they all smiled. "What does that mean?"

"Don't worry about it," Miguel said. "What do you say we go set up Elephant's new cage in your room? Maybe we can connect the new one with the old one, using one of the plastic tunnel tubes to create a hamster mega-mansion."

"Yes!" Angel cheered, holding Elephant close to him again as he hurried up the stairs. "This is the best day ever! I forgive you for missing out on video games, by the way."

"I'm very glad to hear that," Miguel said with a grin, turning to his friends before following Angel up the stairs. "I'll see you around, everyone. Thanks again for all the help."

"Of course," Becca said. "Bye, Miguel!"

Everyone gave their farewells and then gathered at the end of Miguel's driveway. After exchanging high fives and promises to meet up for a clubhouse meeting in the next few days, Kylie took off for her own house, excited to change out of her filthy clothes.

"I'm gonna have so much fun reviewing all this footage and editing it together," Danny said, looking down at the camera that he finally turned off after a long day. "I got so much stuff. And hey, I bet I'm the only one to have filmed the inside of the infamous Gurley Street house before this."

"That's great," Matt said. "Your arm must be killing you after holding that camera up all day."

"Dedication, my friend," Danny answered, flashing Matt and Becca a grin and a peace sign as he walked away. "I do it for the art!"

Then it was just Becca and Matt left.

"What a day, huh?" Becca said, and they slowly made their way over to her house.

"The longest," Matt said. "I'll just pop back into the clubhouse really quick to get Ralphie before I head home."

"I'll go with you," Becca said. "I need to cover that window ASAP. I haven't been able to stop thinking about how the Game Master has been watching us through that telescope! I'll just use thumbtacks to hang up a sheet or something."

"Good idea," Matt agreed as they approached the yard. "Hey, maybe we should get a telescope for ourselves. To spy on the Game Master."

Becca laughed. "We could try, but something tells me that after today, the Game Master is going to find a different hideout."

"Well, hopefully the Game Master won't need another hideout at all," Matt said, uneasy. "Hopefully the game is over, for real this time."

"That'd be so nice," Becca said. "Although I do wish that whoever it was would just reveal themselves already. It's strange to imagine never finding out who did all of this to us."

"It really is."

Just looking at the ladder leading up to the clubhouse made Matt's sore muscles hurt even more, but he needed to get Ralphie down from there. After finding the diagram in the Game Master's notebook about Ralphie, Matt was eager to either reboot or replace the wireless transmitter, hopeful that doing so might help straighten out the problems Ralphie had been facing.

Matt started to climb the ladder, Becca right behind him. "I'm so happy this whole thing is over," he called down to her, just as he climbed into the treehouse. But before Becca could even reply, Matt noticed immediately that something was very wrong in the clubhouse.

"*NO!*" he yelled as he realized that Ralphie was missing. In the place where the robot had been, there was a note, the green GM symbol visible even from across the room.

"What is it?" Becca called up in a panic, scrambling to climb the rest of the way into the room with Matt.

"He's gone," Matt managed. Becca looked at the GM letter and froze in place.

Matt could feel his heartbeat in his face as he dashed across the clubhouse to grab the note that had been left in Ralphie's place.

Matt, the note read in bold letters.

Are you really afraid of heights?